The Mayor's Mission

A Home to Milford College Novel

By Piper Huguley

Liliaceae Press

Cover by JShan

Editors: Gilly Wright and Kiera J. Northington

Dedication

For my students. Always, always remember that you stand on the shoulders of giants.

CHAPTER ONE

Milford, Georgia—April 1868

The hard thuds of a fast horse's hooves on the dry red Georgia clay reverberated through Amanda's body, shaking her awake from a sound sleep. She forced her mind to reason. No. They were not coming for her. Or March. Her father had not sacrificed long and hard to make sure she was educated, so nightriders like Tom Dailey and his boys would come. To get her.

Still, the noise bothered her.

Amanda sat straight up in bed and prepared the rifle next to her to shoot on sight.

Why was that horse coming so fast?

"Stay in your room, March." She called out to her daughter but continued on, unsure if the girl had heard her call or not.

Amanda negotiated the stairs carefully, holding her skirts in one hand and the readied rifle with care in the other. When she got to the bottom, she wiped her hands down the sides of her patched skirt, one at a time. She didn't want the rifle to slip from her hands when she had to shoot.

Then silence.

The hard stomping sounds of the horse stopped. Right in front of her house.

Now, it was up to her to protect everything.

Dear God, please. Be with me. Protect me. Protect March. Protect us all. Amen.

Wet tears slid down her face into the corners of her mouth, and she tasted her own salt and fear.

Those tears might hurt the baby.

A quivering rage filled her fingers and made them shake with hate. She had taken in something that might hurt the new life growing inside of her, an innocent who needed her protection. She hated that she had moved down here and her life would be over today simply because some fool hated the color of her brown skin.

She sniffed up the hate.

No, it wouldn't. Milford College needed her.

March needed her.

The baby needed her.

Virgil needed her. Maybe the most of all.

She pressed her thickening body up close to the closed front door, readying the gun. No. Not today. She would fight with everything she had to protect them all.

A picture flashed in her mind of her dear husband having to lose another wife because he had been away to work.

She stilled her fingers. It had taken her too long to win his love and to reassure him she would be fine in this Georgia wildness.

He would be devastated without her.

Besides, Virgil was too handsome to be lonely for long.

Oh no. She wasn't going anywhere.

She cracked open the door and spoke through the small opening in a loud voice. "You can leave. Nothing here for you but the end of your life if you try to come into this house. God bless you. Be on your way."

Pushing the rifle through the crack of the door, she held it closed with her foot. Whoever it was had not stayed at the hitching post in front, but had moved off to the side of the house, by the barn and probably had not heard her speech.

Was this person a horse thief? Anyone from around here knew her husband had a fair amount of stock, but if she couldn't do anything to protect it . . .

She stepped out onto the wooden porch carefully, trying not to make a sound. Angling her body toward the barn, she pulsed as her heart beat double, both in her chest and in her middle. The thudding of the heartbeats lightened her head.

Was that her baby inside of her?

Her breath came, short and choppy. It seemed as if she had waited so long for the baby to quicken inside her and here it was. At the worst possible time. Still, her hands tingled now with the feeling of love.

Hello, my little one. I love you and I'm going to protect you. Don't you worry. I'm worthy to be your mother.

Protect us, dear Jesus.

She pushed the gun around the corner toward the barn doors to see what fool dared to intrude upon their safety while her beloved husband was not home. Not while she had his child growing underneath her heart . . . she would not fail him. The door opened, and her heart thudded all throughout her body.

"Don't hold up a gun unless you plan to shoot." The lesson from Amanda's father reverberated throughout her mind. Oh yes, she was ready. Every single sense in her body readied to take the life of someone's child to protect her own. She sensed March coming up behind her, and her tall skinny daughter grasped up some of her patchwork skirt and held on.

"Stay still, March."

"Who you shooting at, Mama?" She didn't miss the quaver in March's voice. Her daughter knew what an accurate a shot she was.

"Someone in our barn. Someone came fast down the hill to our house and is in our barn."

"But, Mama, couldn't that be . . .?"

"Hush, child. I need to concentrate. This man won't cause us any trouble."

The door to the barn creaked open, and a large familiar-shaped figure came out.

Virgil. It was her Virgil and he was finally home.

She wilted.

Instantly aware, March had disobeyed one of their primary rules and managed to get herself off their wooden porch and into her father's arms, Amanda straightened up, took the gun out of preparedness mode and hung it on the rack by the door.

Her tears came even faster now as the shape of her dear husband came into view. He bent down, hugging on March and shouting in greeting to all of the excited dogs that ran forward to greet them.

Amanda wanted to smile, wanted to become part of the family reunion scene, but her hands were too slick with sweat.

Before she went back out, she smoothed down her patchwork skirt and the braids of her hair. Would Virgil still think she was pretty? After four months away? With the change in her now? She caught a small glance of herself in the looking glass by the door and frowned. Perhaps not. Her usually smooth braids had frizzed when she had sweated and her round face glowed with her secret. The fear of attack by nightriders, come in the daytime heat of April, shone from her face.

April? What was he doing here now? Last, he said, the Constitutional Convention was going to end by the middle of March and he would be home. Now it was the start of April and there had been no word from him. She frowned more. So relieved to see him, her heart gladdened, but he had some questions to answer. She stiffened her resolve as she walked out of the door. No kissing, no hugging until he would tell her where he was—three weeks late.

When she came out of the front door and he made his way toward the stairs of their home, her feet knew nothing of her resolve. They only wanted to carry her into his arms as fast as possible. She only wanted his thick, juicy lips on hers. Now.

Virgil took her into his arms, smelling of horses, sweat, and bergamot. Dear God, she was so glad to be in his arms again, wrapped around in his heat.

When he put her back down on the ground and reached his mouth down to hers, it was her sweet reward. Any sensible thought flew from her mind as she received his kiss. She still could taste the salt of her tears, mingling with licorice whips, his favorite candy, but she drew him into her, willing him to become part of her so that she would never, ever have to weather the storms of his leave-taking again.

His arms tightened about her, and that's what she liked best, his tight protective hold on her waist pulling her close to him, so tight, near tight as if he would never let her go. And, she liked it that way—liked it fine usually, but there was something else, to think about. Someone else to think about . . .

He broke off their kiss and pulled her from him, eyebrows forming a triangle on his forehead.

She stepped back a little and matched his pitched-up eyebrow look.

Usually in their kissing ritual, there was a part when he would take his big hand and smooth down her braids, grasping the heavy twist of them in his hand, to draw her in just a little bit closer.

She caught her breath when he pulled her from him, quaking inside a bit at the missed part when he would catch her hair in his hand. "Virgil, I . . ."

"Mandy," he commanded in his deep voice. What right did he have not to be happy? He was the one who was three weeks late. Three whole weeks she had to suffer deprived of his love, of his touch. "Mandy, you carrying?"

"Carrying?" Amanda tried to sift through the fog in her brain to know what he meant. She had lived here in the south for almost two years now, but some things . . . words, were beyond her knowledge.

Her husband cut sideways glances up and down the road, grabbing her by her arm as he did so. The only one around was March, laughing and playing with her five dogs in the front yard. "You having a baby?"

Her eyelashes fluttered up and down. She bit the inside of her cheek. Why was he talking to her like this? "Why, Virgil, I can't believe you—well, yes."

He let go of her arm, giving her the stern preacher look he would pull out for couples who had gotten into a whole lot of foolishness before they could get to him to be married.

"Yes? Is that what you saying? Mandy. We had a deal." He pounded a fist on his hand and grasped his hands together, and he struggled to be patient—she knew. "We said . . ."

"I know what we said." She tried to make her voice strong, as she knew it should be, but it quavered. What was the matter with him? "God had a different plan. That happens." She gave a little half laugh and smiled.

Virgil did not smile. Not at all. He stalked off to the barn he had just left, leaving her confused and crying in the middle of the toll road perched at the beginning of Milford proper. The mayor, he was the main law in the town, but he shouldn't accuse her in this way. She didn't know whether to cry or to curse him. Would God blame her if she did both?

His Mandy was all up and down. She always had enough round parts to her to keep her a woman, but she was all angles. She had the skinniest elbows he knew of, especially whenever she would lean on him, staring down at him with her wide eyes, talking into the first morning light over some problem in the town, some way to think about something, something about life.

There would be no more of that now with a baby around.

He forked more hay into Pie's stall. Pie's eyes followed him with concern, like he was crazy since he had just been in there, and Pie didn't need no more food, but he gave her some anyway.

Instead, he stuck the pitchfork in the ground and leaned up on it.

What did she mean these things happen? They had been so careful before he left, making careful use of the envelopes he learned about in the war, taking precious care of her. That was his job. Now he had gone and ruined it all.

He slapped his thigh, but that didn't hurt him enough. What other punishment could he do to himself for getting Mandy in the family way?

He couldn't deny it. Everything over the past few days had been driving him like a dog to get on home so he could bury his face in her braids and feel her skinny elbows digging into his chest with impossible sweet pain.

Now her elbows were fat. Everything about her was round. He could tell the change that overtook her body when he held her to him. There would be no pain when he held her, but he wouldn't be able to have her because of the baby between them.

"Daddy?" March came into the barn quietly looking at him. "What's wrong? You been gone so long, I thought you and Mama would be happy to see one another, and she's crying and you in here hitting on yourself."

Virgil reached down and gathered his girl child in his arms. "I'll go in and help her. She'll be all right."

A flash of memory, long stored away, came to him of having to wash Sally's limp torn- apart body to ready it for the ground. He remembered with some sharp pain, washing away the tears on her face. Tears that had been put there, because she had to leave this world, because of her failure to deliver the large child her new master had put into her body without thought or carc.

Pain knifed his soul in two at the thought the same thing could happen to Mandy.

He gave March another hug. Mandy would be okay. He kissed the braided hair on top of his daughter's head. March was here. Sally had March and she was fine. Why wouldn't that happen for Mandy?

Sally's family surrounded her when she had March, but she didn't have no protection with that other baby. Now because he was away making change, trying to help make a better world for them all, Mandy was in peril in her own body.

Dear God, no.

"Let's go in and help her."

Virgil put the pitchfork carefully away before he could do any more harm to himself. No need of fretting. There would be another baby, that's all.

People always telling him, without Mandy around of course, that he needed a son. They'd been married for two years, almost, and people kept on asking, where was his son?

But, he had a secret.

God blessed him mightily with what he had. His little family was just fine. Didn't need no son. Something happen to him, there were other Baxters here to take care of Mandy and March.

He angled his gaze over the bluff, looking down into Milford proper. Looked fine. Nothing wrong. Amanda kept the school running.

They were fine. They didn't need anything.

See? They didn't need a baby. Amanda would need help with a baby. She couldn't run the school, let alone be in the school with such a heavy load. Still, if there had to be a child, maybe it was better it was now. Looking at her, round as the ripest peach, she'd be having the baby at the end of the summer, in the worst Georgia heat, before school could get started up again.

He grasped March's angular hand, and they climbed the porch steps together. "Go on and play with the dogs now. I'll fix your Mama up."

March did his bidding, as a good daughter should do, and went to play. How would a son do? Whatever he said. That's how it should be around here.

Straightening up, he went into his house to see his wife sitting on the red velvet davenport with her head down, obviously sad.

He approached her with care, noting her curvy body, no slopes no more. And, her front, dear Lord, he hardly recognized her there!

"Umm. Look. Mandy. I shouldn't have said it to you like that. I was only so, I mean, you need to be taking care of the school, and I got the town and well, maybe more of this politics."

He hadn't even told her what happened at the Convention to change the Georgia constitution. What would she say to what she had to tell him—that he was late because there was another potential office, maybe a move to Atlanta . . .

Only Mandy hadn't moved. He stilled, and small sniffling sounds of her snoring and crying in her sleep sounded in the afternoon stillness.

He was nothing but a squashed earthworm underfoot.

He wanted to gather her up in his arms, hold her close to him, but she must need some rest, falling asleep on him in this way.

What could he say to his wife while she was asleep?

Gathering the newly soft Mandy into his arms, he turned to the front of the house and surprised to hear a firm knock on his door. *March wants back in.*

He put his wife back down on the davenport, and opened the door. A strange white man stood there.

He wanted to curse but would not. Preacher men did not curse. Still, the sight of this man at the door was the last thing he expected to see. The news of this baby had shaken him so that he was unprepared—something he never was. Another reason a baby might not work. His head was turned around. In this day and age, a Negro man had to be prepared.

He couldn't reach for his weapon, as he might like, so he used his voice as a gun.

"Who you?"

"Ah, you must be the famous Virgil Smithson. Good to meet you. I've heard so much about you."

The man with greasy brown hair had waxed his moustaches so they stood straight out looking like some bizarre kind of insect wings on his face. His blue eyes lit up like fireflies.

Virgil decided he didn't like him.

"I said, who are you? You got the better of me, and you coming to my door, so you best identify yourself now."

Mandy's small hand touched him on his arm. "Virgil. I told you, this is Robert. Robert Lakey. He's an old schoolmate of mine from Oberlin. He came out to teach in the school. Come in, Robert."

"I hope I wasn't disrupting anything, Amanda."

His wife's beautiful brown face showed her deep dimples, streaked up and down with white salt tracks. Her eyes lit a fiery red like a lantern glow.

"No. Nothing. Come on in." She stepped in front of him to open the door to let this man come in. To their house.

Many an occurrence stuck him as possible. He could believe it when Amanda came into his life. The inheritance of the Milford farm to the community? He could believe, but when Amanda, his darling wife, invited a white man to cross their doorstep as if nothing mattered—as if he didn't matter, that was unbelievable.

An ugly feeling, one he knew and understood was not of God, came up into his hands and he made fists to chase the ugliness away, but it wasn't working.

He and Mandy had a deal, for sure. But, a strange man had entered his home. At Mandy's invite.

Had his beautiful Amanda struck a better deal elsewhere? Found the literate man she had been looking for all her life? Had she had just settled on him, so she could stay in Milford? Who was this Robert person to her? Really?

Virgil went to the davenport and sat down next to Mandy, glaring at the peculiar man who invaded the peace of his home.

He wasn't giving up the goodness he had won, hard fought. No never, not without a fight.

CHAPTER TWO

Retrieving a plate of teacakes and cold teawater, Amanda tried to ignore the deafening silence in the parlor. When she went back in, she stiffened her resolve and tried her best to ignore Virgil's stare at her as she poured drinks and passed around the plate to the men.

Robert grabbed up several of her crumbly peach teacakes in his hand. She brought them out because she knew he loved them. Virgil continued to stare at her as if she had lost her mind for offering their guest anything. Why wasn't he, as a preacher, taking the Christian high road? He should know better.

Rather than giving in to her exhaustion and tiredness at having to defend their home for three extra weeks, she fixed her gaze back at him, with extra intensity, to let him know she had reasons to be unhappy with him too.

She had learned from the best, after all.

She hadn't gotten into this condition all alone, or did he forget about that?

If she could get a baby by herself, she would be the Virgin Mary.

And, he was late. Which he never was. She had feared he was dead. He might have been a messenger bringing her word she was a widow, the last thing she wanted to be.

She set the plate down on the table and grabbed up a teacake, nibbling on the edges to enjoy the sweet, spicy peachy taste. Dried peaches made these taste very well, but as the crumbles melted away on her tongue, she and Virgil stared at one another. Not in passion as when they last met, but something else . . .

No. Not that again.

The glances he gave her did bring back to mind those former glances as he viewed her. His brow furrowed in the same way as he did when she first arrived in Milford, when she was the problem and the unwanted, undesired female teacher.

Well, now he had a male teacher, as he had been trying to get the community for a few years and he couldn't even be civil. Mad at her because she was in a condition she had gotten into—with his help!

Oh, she wanted to cry, but she wouldn't. Bad thoughts in her body and in her blood would impact her child—their child—and she wouldn't harm her baby. Or March. Or him.

"What was the word in the capital?" Robert piped up.

Virgil turned his focused gaze on their guest. Her husband leaned back to relax into a posture that should have made Robert nervous, but he didn't know Virgil well enough yet. He would.

"It's not the capital yet. You go to school with my Mandy?"

"I did. She whupped all of us in those few gentlemen's courses she took. Good thing she took the ladies' course, mostly. I daresay she would have been better than all of us put together. A most extraordinary woman."

"That so?" Virgil leaned forward and selected a teacake in his hand with such masculine grace, her heart skipped a beat as she took a big bite of the dry teacake so that she didn't drool looking at her husband. Curses to him.

I'm sorry. Your Daddy and I aren't getting along just now.

She tried to keep a rein on her emotions for the sake of the child, but some dry teacake would not go down, and she moistened it with a quick sip of teawater. She gulped it down, but it still went down the wrong way because of the haunting image of herself, pressed into her husband's arms.

Robert jumped up and reached over to pat her on the back.

"You all right there, Stew? Can't have anything happen with you now. The school needs your brilliant mind to lead them, eh."

She cleared her own throat and sat up, instantly reacting to this man who put his hands on her. "I'm fine, Robert, thank you."

A hot red shame washed over her, when she realized Robert had touched her. Why had he done that? That had never happened before.

Wiping the smarting tears at the corners of her eyes, Amanda could more clearly see her husband whose eyes narrowed in such a way that she knew his fury was barely contained.

"You have something special to say to Mrs. Smithson?"

"I was trying to ask her about why she felt the attendance of the older children was falling off."

"It's because," Virgil interrupted, with his gaze still firm on Amanda, "it's near harvest time. Since you're from up north and don't know about these things, I'll explain. Folks need a few weeks over this next month to get the cotton in. They'll be back when it is harvested and the fields are empty again. Any other questions?"

She could speak for herself!

She should have spoken for herself!

"That's true," she whispered.

"And now that you have your answer, Mr.?"

"Lakey. Robert James Lakey."

"Certainly." Virgil finished the rest of the teacake in his infuriating calm manner, licking the crumbs from his mouth and moustache with the tip of his tongue with strong, quick licks. "If you'll excuse us, my wife and I need to talk now that I'm back home."

Robert grabbed up another handful of teacakes. Was it her fault her old friend liked her cooking?

"Of course. And, I would love to hear a report from the capital, Virgil. I write for a northern newspaper as well, and they want to know all about how you are here transforming the barbarian south into a place that is equitable for all."

"Of course, Robert," Virgil said in a tone that told her that Robert's lack of respect for her husband's office meant Robert would never get anything from him. "Good day to you."

Virgil did not move from his overstuffed chair, nor did he offer to see the unwelcome guest out.

Amanda stood. "I'll see you in the morning, Robert, and we'll address the situation. If you feel as if you can help me with the small ones, I would appreciate that."

Robert stuffed the buttery cookies in his pocket. "Of course. I'm just letting you know about it, so we can plan accordingly. Good night to you both."

She opened the front door, and March came rushing in with the dogs, nearly knocking Robert down. "So sorry, Mr. Lakey." March called over her shoulder as she ran through to the kitchen.

Amanda waved their guest down to the teacher house, where he lived just down the road from them. She turned to her husband, ready to face him down—strengthened by his blood that she carried inside of her.

"Am I to understand, Mandy, that that man has been here for these months while I was gone?"

"You knew he was coming after Mary Ella got married and left."

"Didn't know he was so familiar with you . . . Stew."

She lowered her head at the old sobriquet. "They called me that because I could cook. And it's part of my last name."

"Your last name," Virgil stood and put his hands in his pockets, showing off his prime male physique, "is Smithson. You best remember that."

She lifted her head. She needed to keep an honor to her husband, but he had it all wrong here, and he needed to know. "Of course. And, you can remember I'm carrying a Smithson. Or do you want to forget that?"

Virgil squared his shoulders and stood next to her. "I need to check on the smithy. Don't wait up for me. You need rest. Especially in your state. Excuse me."

He plowed past her, leaving her with no hug, no kiss. Nothing. Just a regard for her state.

Only after he left, did she dare sag into his overstuffed chair, hot tears squeezing from her eyes, wanting to be embraced by him instead of the chair he had so recently occupied.

After he threw himself on Pie's back, Virgil let the horse have free rein carrying him across the countryside far away from Milford almost to Crumpton on the other side of the toll road. Fool thing to be coming out here in the near darkness, but he needed to be somewhere where he could be alone, instead of thinking about how some fool white man dared to put his hands on his wife.

Old greasy head. Lucky he didn't kill him. But, he had no time to take up with a foolish schoolmaster. Too many problems, too much change was happening in the state. He had to make sure that Mandy and March were ably protected. There was so much to do, so much more travel to do; that meant he would be away and yet, here was that schoolmate of hers, sniffing around, calling her Stew and such.

She only married you to have a place to go.

The old ugly thoughts popped up in his head, and he turned Pie back to Milford. No use of him being out with the nightriders. He needed to do as he said, go to his smithy to make sure Isaac had taken good care of it. But, he knew his good friend had done as he should.

No, he needed to get back to his wife and find out from her what was going on, talk to her about future options for funding her school, but his pride caught him square up in the throat.

He would have never believed it if someone had told him this, all would be what he found when he returned home.

Dear God, help me to know what to do.

Swallowing the pride he knew to be a vanity, God did not disappoint him. Just a quick stop at the smithy would help.

When he rode into the town square of Milford toward the smithy, it did not help him to forget his wife. Every tree, every pink and red flower that edged the town square, where his smithy sat on the far side, sang of Amanda. Her touch and her loving influence on his little hamlet was everywhere all at once, as if she were holding the town in her arms.

Who was he fooling?

He could strut about like a Banty rooster all he wanted; it was clear who was the real mayor of Milford. And, he was not embarrassed by that. Instead, her capability to take care of things on her own . . . pleased him. What a fine woman he had married. What a fool he was wandering around the town square, surrounded by frilly spring flowers that edged with a flagpole and nice spring grass planted up in the red dirt. Instead of doing the sensible thing, he guided Pie down into the valley where he saw Isaac, his friend, who was in charge of his smithy now, about to close the door.

His face contorted, like March's when she ate something she didn't like. In a further rebuke to him, Isaac hugged his wife, Pauline as she came to greet him in the smithy. They acted as if they were the ones separated for months. He shook his head. These public shows were just not appropriate. He was glad for Isaac and Pauline, but did they have to be so open?

Isaac turned and pointed at him, sitting high up on Pie. He stepped away from his wife, but still held on to her hand. "Boss man! You back. So good to see you."

Isaac extended his hand out to Virgil, but kept a firm hold on Pauline as they shook hands. He knew his priorities.

Pauline, however, was always able to see through him. Her eyebrows came together in the middle of her forehead. "You been home yet?"

"I have."

"Why ain't you still there?"

Virgil straightened up higher on his horse. "I had some things to check on down here in the valley."

Pauline waggled her finger. "No. No, that's not it. You been fussing at Amanda. Haven't you?"

Isaac drew back from the aftermath of their handshake. "Pauline, that's not it, I'm sure." He turned back to Virgil. "The smithy's fine. We can square things in the morning, boss."

"Isaac Baxter, when you going to learn to listen to your wife? They done had a fight. I can smell it on him, like burnt bacon."

"I'll go home now." Virgil prepared to turn Pie back homeward. He didn't need this.

"What would he be fighting with Amanda for? They been apart for months. He love his wife." Isaac had developed into a good smithy in his training, but sometimes, his reasoning was not as sharp as his wife's. Good thing Pauline had him firm in hand. God had provided well for him as a mate.

God had provided well for him too, but he was not showing his gratitude, as he should. A sinking feeling roiled in his stomach. He thought he really should go home and make things right with Mandy, instead of feeding on it.

"'Bout to be an election. Georgia said they would do it, so we had to line it up so Georgia can get back into the Union. Lot to do to make that."

"Isn't that something?" Isaac reared back.

"It is. So we got to prepare."

"Glory be! What you going to do now?"

"I came home to get some more things and go back to the capital. I come home, and things changed."

"That the real problem, isn't it?" Pauline's hand pulled from her husband's, and she peered up at Virgil in the dusk. "Amanda carrying and you feeling sorry you can't do what you need to do over all of this political foolishness. They ain't never going to let us have more than what we got, Virgil, when are you going to get some sense?"

"Pauline, we've got to try."

"Bad times been around for so many years, you think they going to roll over and give it all up to us? All at once?" Pauline stepped to Pie and petted his nose. The way she could show tenderness at the most unexpected times always surprised him.

"I wasn't saying that. They letting us have power. Got to get things done before they change their minds."

"Fool man. Wake up. It's not happening all at one time. Meanwhile, you down here talking to us, and your wife need you. She been waiting for you for weeks and wanting you to come."

"'Cause she carrying."

"What of that? It's God's blessing. If I could . . ."

The carelessness of his words hit him full on in the face. Pauline couldn't have children. She had gotten hurt on the inside many years ago. Mrs. Milford's doctor, herself, told her so.

"I wasn't expecting it. That's all."

"I thought she wrote and told you. You didn't get her letter?"

"I can read now. I know what she said, but some of what she said didn't make sense. Maybe that's what she was trying to say."

Pauline shook her head. "Guess someone as high raised as Miss Mandy can't write that stuff down directly. Bless her."

Virgil didn't understand why she just couldn't have said it straight out in the letter. What good was knowing how to read and write if things just couldn't be said?

"You tell her you happy?" Pauline's eyes narrowed on him.

"Not exactly." Virgil tightened his hold on the reins to keep Pie still.

"What you mean by that?" Isaac peered at him now. He sure didn't mean to stir him up. His former apprentice, and now partner, let Virgil have the lead in everything, but if something was to make Mandy and March, his blood nieces, unhappy, he wouldn't stand for it—Virgil knew.

"Don't know how I'm feeling about it."

"There ain't no way to feel about it but happy." Isaac informed him with some smithy steel in his voice.

"Tell him, husband."

He spoke up. "We had a deal. We was supposed to . . . can't say. Just, she got too much on her plate to be having a baby."

"And you ain't at fault?"

"Maybe I ain't. I go up there and see that teacher man with his hands on my wife. Maybe . . ."

"Oh Lord. Jesus, take me to the cross." Pauline waved her arms in the air and Isaac grabbed up Pie's reins himself.

"You best get down off of that horse and look me in the eye if you saying something like that about my niece." Isaac pulled the horse closer to him.

"I'm tired. I don't know what I'm saying." The air went out of his lungs now that he had spoken his fears out into the open. His body sagged, but a renewed energy infused his veins. Seeing their reactions, he could see how ridiculous his fears were. He knew Amanda would never . . . he knew that. But, when he saw that man with his hands on her, helping her not to choke. . .

Please, God, take these bad feelings out of my heart and mind. Help me now.

"Boss. I'm going with my wife now. You need to go home to your wife and search your heart about what you just said. It's late, and you tired, having ridden all day and with the news about the election."

"You all are right and I . . ."

"My husband is right," Pauline edged closer to Isaac. "Take yourself on home. You be feeling better in the morning. I don't have to tell you that Miss Mandy has been every inch the lady while you was gone. I suspect you know that. And you know don't no one stepping on this earth mean more to her than you, less it was March and that little baby she carrying. You better respect that and stop worrying about deals you two had. That's over. New day ahead."

"You right, Pauline."

"You better believe it." She turned away from him, pulling Isaac after her, muttering on the edge of her breath. "Didn't worry about no deals when he got what he wanted off of her.

"I'ma see you in the morning, Boss man. Mind be cleared then. Go on."

Isaac and Pauline went into the darkness, hands clasped, murmuring together about his craziness and how this political stuff might not benefit their folks anyway—look at what it was doing to him.

Maybe it had made him crazy.

Everything in this latest success in the wake of the Convention to fix a date for an Election Day drove him to come back to his Mandy, where he felt as if he could do anything.

He needed her by his side.

His heart took up residence in his throat to think about the possibility of losing his Mandy. Then it would all be his fault—because they made a mistake one night before he left and didn't use an envelope like their deal said.

Lord, help me. I didn't mean to. I didn't . . .

He guided Pie up the hill to the bluff where their stone-built house overlooked his town. He rode poor, tired Pie a little faster than usual into the stable, and took a little time to settle her in and gave her extra feed for as hard as she had worked to get him home to his family.

No more ingratitude toward the women in his life.

Time to admit he was wrong. Instead of dreading admitting it to her, he took an extra brisk step to his house.

He couldn't wait to have Amanda in his arms again.

CHAPTER THREE

Covering her baby with a protective hand, Amanda laid on the wooden bed that her husband had hewn with his own hands.

No wonder he had reacted so strangely. He had reacted that way because he didn't know about the baby.

She had written it in her letters, but had she been clear enough for someone who had been completely illiterate as recently as two years ago? She had just assumed Virgil had completely overcome his illiteracy, but even as fast as he had been learning, she should have known. It takes time to learn. She should have simplified her language more. She should have known better. What kind of teacher was she anyway?

The kind who needed a lesson or two.

A hot tear dripped off the end of her nose into the pillow. Might as well go to sleep while she waited . . .

The front door downstairs opened, and the familiar footfall of her husband trudged up the stairs. Her heart surged out of old habit at hearing him come up to the bedroom. He would come in here with her. He still loved her.

She wanted to sit up, but a small wave of nausea prohibited her from sitting up too quickly.

"Your papa is coming," she whispered to the baby. "He wants to say hello."

Virgil stood in the doorway and stopped. Was he staring down at her? Frowning at her roundness? Her shape shifted into a different way lately. She had liked it, but what if he didn't?

She turned over to view him and her stomach clenched. Would he give her his thundercloud look again? Like God's wrath? Peering at him in the darkness, that wasn't what she saw.

He just stood there, hands in his pockets, brow furrowed, puzzled as she knew he could be, but not angry.

"I was trying to get an Election Day organized."

Oh. Not what she was expecting. So, he had something to deal with as a start. She righted herself easily, gradually, so the nausea didn't come up on her so fast.

Well, that didn't work. She reached for the tin pan she kept close by these days and quietly threw up the remains of the rabbit stew she had made for dinner.

Rabbit stew was something that babies would not like. She should have known better.

"Dear God, Mandy!"

Virgil ran out of the room and down to the kitchen, she knew, to get a cold cloth for her.

Except he did better than that. He thoughtfully bought her a mug of fresh water. "Swish that in your mouth and spit in the pan."

She did as he directed her, and without hesitation, he carried the pungent smelling pan outside.

She felt better now that her dinner was gone from her. She arranged herself to look pretty when he came back into the room again, so he needn't worry about her.

Virgil rested the freshly rinsed tin pan next to her. "You feeling all right?"

"Not really. I've been worried about you."

He frowned. "It ain't right for you to still be so sick. When's this baby going to come?"

"Pauline say August."

"You need a regular doctor, not old Pauline."

"I'll be fine."

Virgil sat on the bed next to her, as if she were a china doll, afraid to touch her. She wished he wasn't. Maybe if she talked about what he needed to discuss. "Why did it take so long?"

"'Cause of the White Democrats. Said Republicans of any color wasn't welcome, but they'd tolerate the scalawag white ones."

"Scalawag?" Amanda screwed up her face as she said the strange word.

"The ones what are helping the enslaved. Mrs. Milford would be one, if she was still living."

Mandy nodded. "I suppose so."

"We don't have to take it. Making up our own meeting in Valdosta."

She peered at him. "Wonderful! When?"

Her husband averted his eyes away from her. "August."

She gave a small half laugh. "I would expect so. You're going to be leaving me again. And, they want money for the taxes on the property. In August."

Now it was her husband's turn to half laugh. "'Course. When else?"

She leaned in to him, and he didn't move away from her. She encircled his neck, fully prepared to hug up on him. "I'm sorry. I know we had a deal."

He sure took his time about holding her again, but he did, and she relaxed in his strong, secure hold, as she liked to do. "I'm mad for myself, Mandy, too. You in this way . . . it was my fault. It's my job to protect you, and I failed you."

"I know when it happened," she whispered. "Right before you left. I didn't want to let you go. I was willing to do anything to have you closer to me. Anything to keep you as part of me. I was a little too successful."

"Yes, wife. You do all things well, as I have come to know. I'm just sorry. I wanted you to come with me this time. Meet the other ones of us trying to change things. And now . . ."

"There'll be another time."

She reached up to stroke his trimmed beard. Soft and pliable. He watched her hand as she stroked his face. "Mandy, maybe you oughtn't."

He grabbed at her wrist. "I don't think it's the thing to do now."

"I want to."

"Well, I don't want you to."

"Touch you? My own husband?"

She thought his deep thundercloud voice caused her to stir. She didn't like it any better when he spoke to her in this low terrible way.

He sprang up away from her. "I'll sleep in the guest room."

"There's no bed ties on the post." There had been no need for any since she was the guest two years ago.

"I'll put some on. Won't take but a minute."

"You belong in here, with me."

"Mandy. Don't ask me to do that."

"Sleep with your wife? As God requires?"

"I been waiting for four months. I don't know if I can . . ." Why wouldn't he look at her? What was he talking about?

"You need to do your marital duty by me, Virgil."

"I get in that bed with you, wife, I don't know if I can be responsible for what I do. Now, you got something to protect, you need to be about protecting it and not thinking basely."

"Pauline said it would be okay."

"You talking to Pauline about our marriage bed?"

Mandy nodded her head. "You aren't the only one who's been waiting for four months, Virgil."

The tension tightened around his beautiful mouth, and he ran out of the room as if fire were on his tail.

He didn't even bid her a good night.

****

This was not what he thought he was coming home to. Slapped-around grits and red eye gravy on a plate. A little of the brown gravy sloshed over on the tablecloth, and Mandy didn't even bother to wipe it up as she shoveled in food like she had just come from the fields.

March was the one who saw his displeasure and got a cloth to wipe up the spilled gravy with. Who was this woman he had married?

He would try to be nice now.

"You was right, Mandy. Bed ties needed a little fastening. I'll take care of that when I get home."

"You don't need to worry about bed ties if you're sleeping in the right bed."

Well, he probably deserved that. He shook his head to clear it some.

"I'll check ours as well."

"No need. I took care of that while you were gone. I needed the bed to be tight for my back, since it hurts some times."

He steeled himself so he didn't wince. Pain? In her back? His Mandy? For carrying?

He wanted to stand and offer her some salve they used at the smithy to ease their muscles. Pauline made the stuff for Isaac, and Isaac shared with him. The look on her face was so cross; he didn't know what to say. Scraping the last of the grits from his plate, he stood. "I'll get started. I can take March on with me."

"I'm going too." Mandy reproached him. "I have to get down to the school."

"It's okay, Daddy. Mr. Lakey walks with us to the schoolhouse."

Virgil gripped an edge of the table. *Do God.* His favorite line from his favorite field song echoed in his head over and over until he felt like an ache was coming on. First thing when he got to the smithy, he would rub some of that salve on his forehead. It was good everywhere.

"I see. Don't let me disrupt your patterns."

"Virgil, you're welcome to come with us."

"I'm a need to ride Pie in anyway. Probably got mayor business all around. Anything I should know about?"

"Not that I know of. Ride around on Pie, and let people know you are back."

"I do that then. While you go walking with Mr. Lakey." He didn't mean for his words to sound harsh, but they just came out that way. The pained look showed because the dimples went away. It was enough to wound him. He watched her ease herself up, a little off balance, to clear the table of dishes, so she could get on with her morning of teaching the little ones to read and write.

Or was she running to meet with Mr. Lakey?

He had things to do as well.

He stood up and strode out to the barn to get Pie ready to go. There was a stirring outside, and the high, sweet sounds of Mandy's voice rang out to him, her voice greeting Mr. Lakey with cheer and good feeling. The way she used to greet him.

His midsection hurt for the feeling of her directing that voice toward him, even before he had come to see her for the light she was in his life. What had he ever been before she came to Milford as a mistake?

She had been no mistake. God had provided this woman to lighten his load in life. To be a comfort to him. What did he do with that gift but to question it? No wonder she was mad at him.

Still, her voice.

He waited until the sounds of their voices retreated enough so he wouldn't run into them on the road, the same road he was taking to go into the valley. Pie took the pace at a canter, seeing March and Mandy up ahead, walking with Mr. Lakey. March danced and pranced about, as she always did. Mandy walked with slow, steady steps. She was still upright and dignified in spite of her burden. Love for her exploded in the middle of his chest and expanded throughout him in a burst of warmth.

Still, he felt some horror at her walking around with the greasy Robert Lakey. What was with the man's grooming? He had built everything as state of the art in the teacher house. Was he making use of the bathing rooms?

He needed to.

Instead of love, a surge of anger swelled. If Mandy wanted to spend time with a fool, that was up to her.

He recalled the other fool in her life he owed money too—Mr. Charles Henry. He had almost finished paying off the note he had signed off on almost two years ago, the note that was the surety of Amanda's true liberty even as Mr. Lincoln had freed the slaves. A lot of people felt the deceased Mr. Lincoln had not been in the right interfering with their loans and payoffs of the formerly enslaved, and they still wanted the money they were owed. Henry had been a staunch abolitionist, but he still wanted his money.

He would get every penny he was owed for the freedom of his wife. She would be free.

"Ho there, Virgil. A fine April day isn't it? The kind that Robert Burns wrote about in some of his fine poetry."

No, Lord. Was this fool about to spout poetry at him? Tempted to get off of Pie to kneel at the side of the road to pray he wouldn't, he gripped the reins harder instead.

“I don’t know anything about who Robert Burns is. I just want to let you know I’ma be taking on the duty of escorting my wife and daughter to school from now on.” He laced Pie’s reins lightly through his fingers, and stared straight ahead while addressing the strange man who wrote poetry. The reins got to feeling slick. This fool was dumb enough to try to trick him, no doubt. He didn’t like it.

“I understand. Now that you are back.”

He glanced at the man sideways. If he had been in the man’s place, and it was about Mundy, he wouldn’t have given up so easily. Had he misjudged the man’s regard for his wife?

No. He hadn’t. Robert Lakey’s sliding features filled with confusion. No doubt, the man would miss the mornings, walking down to the former Milford farmhouse, where classes were held, talking about some poetry nonsense with his wife.

“Good.” He resumed looking ahead. “I’m the law in this hamlet, and I wouldn’t want to have to arrest you on indecency or theft. Good day.”

He urged Pie into a faster trot, and now March’s face filled with confusion flashed before him, as she held her mother’s hand and walked as a young lady of eight should. Most striking of all was his wife’s look at him, eyebrows drawn together and peaked up. Was she feeling okay? Did she need the basin again? Maybe he should be taking her in the wagon, but the walk in the fresh spring sunshine couldn’t have hurt her. Or could it?

Maybe she was angry with him for his suggestion.

He had made sure to direct his warning words to Robert Lakey, not Mandy. To show he was not accusing her of anything, only Lakey. Surely, she could see that.

She's with child, man. Will she be able to see reason in anything?

His uncertainty made his chilled fingertips stiff in the warm day and threatened to freeze the reins to his hands.

He hoped so.

Instead of riding around town that morning, he went to the smithy to help Isaac. Staying at the smithy meant he would be close to the Milford farmhouse, close to Mandy if she wanted to come and talk to him.

Almost at midmorning, he looked up. Sometimes she walked over at recess to talk to him, but Mandy had not come to talk to him yet. Was she ignoring him because of how he had confronted Lakey? Her old school chum?

He rubbed his hands near the fire of the smithy. Probably. Even Isaac was more quiet than normal. Shaking his fingers out, he opened his mouth to talk it over with Isaac.

Then he stopped.

Isaac should see reason. What was the matter with him? Was he letting family feelings get in the way of what he knew was right? What if some white man wanted access to his Pauline? How would he feel about that?

He knew better than to bring it up to him like that. Old times weren't so long ago that a white man helping himself to his wife wasn't a distinct impossibility.

Which was the exact reason why he didn't like Lakey acting as if he had rights to "Stew."

The whistle of the once a day train sounded and both men stopped their activity. The train would stop in Milford this morning for some reason. Deliveries? Mail? Visitors?

"Someone coming," Isaac said in a direct way.

"Think so?"

"Train stopping too long for just cargo."

He hadn't been away so long that he didn't get Isaac's point. Well, if someone new was in town, he needed to be about greeting them.

He took off his blacksmith apron, donned his black frock coat, and prepared his tie. "I'll need to see who's coming on through here. I'll be back later on. You okay?"

"Held things down while you was gone all those months. I'm fine."

Virgil fit the coat onto himself. Why did people need to remind him of how long he had been gone? He knew it. Why were people giving him a hard time about it as it was? He had been gone trying to make things better for all of them, and people did not seem to appreciate it. Maybe when they had the election, they would see.

He had no time to reflect on that. With sure strides, he made his way downhill to the train platform to see who had come into Milford.

Rounding the corner, he encountered two ladies on the platform. They were both dressed in the very best fashion of the day. One of them, a blonde-haired lady wore a royal blue dress with hoops as wide as his Amanda's the first day she came to Milford. She spoke to the other, "I'd rather we came by carriage, Clara. The train ride was awful."

"Better that we come by train, Lucy." The one with dark black hair and eyebrows said, smoothing down her own purple dress. "We've wasted enough time already."

Virgil's heart raced in his chest. Clara and Lucy. The Milford daughters-in-law. Ever since the day the Milford property had passed onto to the Smithsons for the purposes of establishing a school, he had lived in fear of this day. Now it was here.

It's a good thing I'm here to help with it.

The arrival of Clara and Lucy meant trouble sure enough.

And Clara, the one with the dark hair that the former slaves called demon lady, because of the strange high arch of her eyebrows, saw him. "Hey, yes. There's help. Come and fetch our travel valises, you. Over here."

Lucy turned her wide skirts around to see him. "Oh my dear Clara. Don't you know Virgil when you see him? He was Mother's favorite, don't you recall?"

Virgil stepped forward. "Yes, Mrs. Milford. I remember you. Good to see you again."

The steam rising off of Clara seemed apparent as she evaluated this little scene. "Yes. I remember him. And Mother is dead now, Lucy. You must know that. And Virgil here knows what to do with our valises as well."

He turned to her and as he might have never done in the old times, fixed his gaze on her and stared at her. And she, bold baggage as she was, stared right back at him.

Had the bad times come back so quick?

CHAPTER FOUR

Amanda kept her basin on the desk in front of her. Even as she sat to hear students recite, the tin pan was a blessing to her. She had one here and one at the house, always at the ready.

What have I ever done to deserve this?

For the first time in a while, a fleeting thought of her mother came into her mind's eye. Was this how it had been for Aurelia Stewart? Such a struggle to bring life forward?

She knew she had passed the life span of her mother some months ago, and the keen sense of disappointment rose in her as a pang to her heart that she had not known her.

"Thank you May," she told the little girl with pigtails who recited in a high-pitched voice. The sweet child beamed and went back to her seat.

The recitations finished, she should have gotten up to teach something else, but the heat of the day kept her in her teacher's chair.

She picked up a slate and waved it in front of her face. "Hot day, isn't it? Did the train stop?"

"It sure did, Mama. I mean Mrs. Smithson."

March knew better, she knew what to call her at the school.

"I wonder who it is."

March glided to the window. "I can't see a thing. They may be coming here directly." The child shrunk back at Amanda's directed gaze at her boldness in getting out of her seat without permission.

"Meanwhile," Amanda pressed a hand to the desktop so she could stand, "there's work to be done."

Thirty pairs of eyes fixed on her as she stood to teach another lesson of subtraction. Something else, a power beyond herself directed her to sit back down.

Powerless to resist, she obeyed. Her body was not her own these days.

"How about an exercise break? Let's go outside and enjoy the fresh April air."

She kept her voice upbeat for the sake of the children, but she really wanted some of that good April air herself.

No one needed to tell the children twice. This classroom, formerly the parlor, was situated right next to the front door, so the children were more than ready to leave and play in the large front yard of dirt that extended all the way up to the train tracks.

March lingered after the children ran out.

She frowned at her young daughter. This was not like her. March led the children's games. The stuffiness of the schoolhouse trampled on March's natural energies, and she usually would have been the first one out of the door.

"What are you going to do now, Mrs. Smithson?"

Amanda moved gingerly to the door. March reached out to clasp her hand, and she took it. "I'll sit on the porch in the rocking chair while you go play. Go on ahead."

A stormy frown sat on March's brow. "You want me to get Daddy? Or Mr. Lakey?"

"Certainly not." Having reached the front porch, she eased herself into the rocking chair, well placed in the shade. A small, but strong breeze stirred off the inlet nearby. The feel of the air on her face restored her soul. Was this how March felt being confined in a classroom all day? "You play. Just as I told you."

March danced off into the yard with the other children, leaving her mother, and her cares, behind.

Amanda smoothed a hand down her front, where the baby stirred, probably also stirred by the breeze. She wanted nothing more than to take a nap, but she knew she couldn't. How did women do this? It might have been a good reason why the American Missionary Society didn't allow married women to teach in the classroom. Lately, though, they had to loosen that restriction. There was so much work to be done, so many of the formerly enslaved, who needed the help of ones just like her. So, she couldn't take a break, no matter how much she wanted to. What a blessing to have the help of Robert.

Mr. Lakey.

It was hard to think of her old school chum in such a formal way, but given the way her husband had acted at him yesterday, she'd better.

She sniffed at Virgil's overreaction yesterday. Where had all of that come from? He knew she had given up everything for him, to be here with him, to help him in this mighty work they both had started. How could he believe she would do anything to jeopardize that?

If anything, she should be the one asking questions about where he had been—coming home three weeks late. Maybe he had been the one to find someone else, someone prettier, someone who was more used to his southern way of life . . .

She pushed the ridiculous thought from her. Virgil's stormy good looks were certainly enough to attract the attention of many women, but she knew him, deep in her heart. His moral code meant, once he loved, he loved deeply and completely. It was the honor of her life to be the recipient of his singular and intense devotion, yet why did he behave so strangely?

She embraced herself at the thought of having been on the receiving end of that love, wishing, somehow, she could receive that love again without his anger at her situation.

"You feeling okay, Stew?"

Robert Lakey appeared over her shoulder and looked out of the window at his class of six older students who were getting their own recess break.

She sat up, straighter in the chair, coloring. It was not seemly of her to be thinking impure thoughts about her husband in the middle of the day. Still the additional warmth to her face made the tears start in the corners of her eyes, and she brought a handkerchief out of her pocket. How could he ever think her desiring another man? Did he not see, or care about the way she felt about him?

She blew her nose and hoped that would clear her mind. "I'm fine."

"Wonderful idea to let the students come outside. Beautiful day."

"It is." The wind stirred around and despite her intense desire to sit down, Amanda braced herself to stand, and Robert Lakey helped her to her feet. Sure enough, from the direction off to the east of Milford's small depot came a party of people, including her husband who looked none too pleased at carrying several suitcases while wearing his good dark brown broadcloth suit.

Amanda frowned. She would be the one scrubbing out the sweat stains from under his arms. He should have gotten the wagon to carry luggage.

Then she noticed the two ladies coming behind him.

Immediately she noticed how much smaller their skirts were, and envy stirred in her breast, along with the shifting child. Those were the fashions this year. Oh, how nice it would be to have a pretty dress in the latest fashion. The taller lady with blue-black hair was dressed in an intense lavender dress, and had the cutest hat perched upon her head, tied on with ribbons of the deepest blue violet.

The other lady, a blonde carrying a child in a white dress, came behind her. She was shorter and wore a royal blue print dress sprigged with spring flowers. Their clothes were lovely, but their apparel stirred a protective feeling in her and she couldn't say why.

The children stopped playing immediately and March came to her side, her bare feet pounding a beat on the wooden steps of the house as she went to her mother.

"Do you know those ladies, March?"

"The Milford daughters. First pretty one there is Miss Clara, she was married to young Mr. John, and second one is Miss Lucy. She married to Mr. Frank."

"Your husband looks as if he needs some assistance . . ." Robert Lakey stepped forward to Virgil, and she could see that her husband did not know how to receive his offer of assistance. He ignored Lakey and went to the porch.

Virgil put down all four of the cases he carried and stepped off the porch. She exhaled a breath she did not know she held, relieved to see his exertions had not dirtied his clothes as much as she feared.

"I would never know the place now." The one dubbed Miss Clara by March had a loud honking voice. She stood in front of them all with a hand on her hip.

Why was everyone so quiet?

"Good morning ladies," Robert said to Clara and bowed deeply at the waist.

"Well, at least there is someone white here. It's not as bad as I thought, even with Negroes sitting on Mama's front porch."

Amanda grabbed up some of her patchwork skirt in her fist. Her feelings were already stirred up because of the new clothes that these women wore.

"They're resting in the shade Clara. It's a hot day," the one named Lucy piped up. Lucy clearly was no wilting flower herself and she carried a small grip of her own, as well as the small child, and set them both down.

Clara carried nothing and had nothing that was interesting. March told her long ago that there were Milford granddaughters. Where were they? She stepped down off the porch to greet the women.

"Welcome to Milford College. I'm afraid some of the Baxters have the advantage of me, for they seem to know you, but I don't."

Clara put her hands on her hips. "Where did you come from?"

She drew in a breath, supposing Clara's question came from the way that she spoke and sounded in contrast to the Baxters. She ignored the question. "I'm Amanda Smithson."

"Smithson?" Clara frowned. "Why does that sound familiar?"

Lucy nodded. "It's Virgil's name. She must be his wife." Lucy nodded her head to Amanda and she gave her greeting back.

She didn't like the way that Clara regarded her, so she informed her. "Yes and I'm the lead teacher here."

"The school is in the house?"

Clara looked toward the edifice. "Well, that won't do. It's a house. No wonder it looks so different. Where are we to stay then? In the slave cabins? Heavens, there must be a hotel in Crumpton by now. It's such a backwater here."

"It was your idea to come, Clara." Lucy stepped forward to the porch and guided her child up to the shade. The boy's beauty touched Amanda's heart as his brown curls danced all over his head.

His baby beauty made her arms ache to hold her own baby as he sat in his beautiful white dress, on the step. He made himself comfortable by picking up a stick and poked at the iron red clay of Georgia with it, but his mother didn't mind at all.

She gathered herself and said, “There are still bedrooms in the house. We hold class in the parlor and in the larger sitting room upstairs only.”

“Thank God.” Clara intoned. “I just couldn’t fathom staying elsewhere.”

“Would you ladies like some refreshment on this hot day?” Robert waved a hand and one of his pupils went inside to the kitchen.

Amanda could see that Clara threw him a relieved look. “Thank you, sir.”

“I’m Robert Lakey. Principal of this institution. Please, come and sit.”

He guided them up onto the porch and sat Clara in the rocking chair Amanda had just vacated. Lucy sat in the small non-movable chair next to it.

She grabbed up some of her skirt. *Dear God. Help me with my patience and giving.*

Seeing Clara sitting there in the chair she just left, and a young woman hurrying forward with two cool glasses of lemonade made something stir in Amanda’s stomach. It wasn’t the baby. What was the complete story on these women anyway? School would probably have to be dismissed due to the intrusion of these visitors. She took on a Virgil frown, at the sight of these invaders come to ruin the peace of the school day.

“I’ve got to get back to the smithy.” Virgil boomed out to break up the quiet as Lakey settled the women on the porch. Having him around seemed to serve a purpose. Maybe he was helpful in some way after all. Long as he kept his eyes and hands to himself.

Mandy came down off the porch and put her arm through the crook of his. "I need you here with me, Mr. Mayor."

"Don't know why. You seem to have it all in control. Like normal."

What had Young Mr. John seen in devil woman? She was such a big, tall woman. He knew her people were from Tennessee, and that they had come from nothing. Clara came up in the world when she had managed to get Mr. John to marry her. For only one reason. He frowned.

March stepped forward to the old devil woman. "Ma'am. You didn't have Miss Genevieve and Miss Rose with you?"

Clara Milford's eyes did not take in his daughter. "No," her voice rang a little sharp. "They're in school just now. Where good little girls belong."

Mandy stepped forward. "March was in school herself just now, until the interruption to her day. You may go, dear."

He had never seen his child move so fast. Or Mandy say anything less than something charitable to anyone. Seems as if the baby had changed things in his wife's Christian demeanor, as well as in her appearance. He didn't have as much town business as he thought he did.

He lifted a lapel of his day coat and let a bit of the breeze blow close to his shirt. He did not like the appearance of this little scene, with the white people up on the porch as in the bad old times, and he and Amanda standing in the dirt as if they were ready to serve. He wanted to put at least his foot up on the steps, but the little shaver was there, playing in the dirt about to get his white dress dirty.

Must be Mr. Frank's son. Cute baby—seemed well mannered too.

But, they all started out with good manners. 'Til they got to know who they was in the world.

"Who authorized a school here?" Clara demanded as she sipped on her cool teawater.

Virgil made a gesture with his hand, and one of the young women, Liza, came to him. "Could you bring us lemonade too, Liza? You see how it is with Mrs. Smithson in the sun."

"Yes, sir." Liza said and went back into the back of the house in the kitchen.

He took Mandy's arm and guided her back up onto the porch to another chair, a bit away from the other two.

"Hope you ladies don't mind. Mrs. Smithson is expecting a happy event in a few months' time. Don't want her to get to feeling bad."

Lucy smiled at him. "That's wonderful, Virgil. Congratulations."

"Hmm."

Demon lady was not at all happy at the prospect of sitting on the porch with his wife, but she was just going to have to deal with it. The bad old days were over.

"How long will you lovely ladies be with us, here?" Lakey asked them, taking a plate of cookies from the tray Liza carried back out with their lemonade on it.

Clara sipped again. "This is our home. We have nowhere to go."

Lucy spoke up. "Well, that's not quite true, Clara. You have your family in Tennessee."

"It's as true as I'm going to make it." She snapped at her sister-in-law.

"Why did it take you so long to come back?" Mandy reached for the cold tin mug Liza brought her, and Virgil was glad to see his wife's appearance perk up some more at the sips of the lemonade she took in.

"So long? Excuse me?" Clara stared at Mandy as if she had no right to speak.

"After the war, Mrs. Milford." Lakey clarified.

"Several things were going on in Tennessee that had to be settled. It's really none of your concern."

"I see." He took a swig of his own lemonade and felt restored. "I thought it was just that you were used to not visiting here in Georgia. Since you all haven't been here more than a handful of times."

"It's my own beloved's homeland. I can't see it degenerate into a pile of wood."

"It's being taken care of, Mrs. Milford, as you can see." Virgil provided to her.

"And to see about its ownership. It's well understood Mama was slipping away into insanity at the end of her life. The thought that she would leave this place to a bunch of . . . you, is just ridiculous. We came to right a wrong."

Lucy lowered her head and called out to her child not to put the stick in his ear. "We needed to see what happened to her at the end."

"She died with God's word on her lips." Mandy let her know. "Asking for his forgiveness."

Clara hooted. "Forgiveness, for what?"

"For the crime of holding people in the chains of slavery."

Clara waved her hand and set down her empty glass. "That's exactly as I mean it. She was crazy. No one needed to ask forgiveness of that. If that were the case, everyone in these United States would need forgiveness over this insane war that killed my John and her Frank."

"Maybe it occurred to her what the war was really about." Mandy leveled at Clara.

Clara turned to her. "You never said where you come from, Mrs. Smithson."

"Ohio. Two years ago."

"A Yankee. Isn't that something? Did you ply your trade before?"

"I certainly did not. I was in college."

"College? You mean to tell me you have a college degree?"

"I certainly do."

"Well, now I've heard everything."

"I went to college with Mrs. Smithson." Lakey volunteered, and Virgil had another reason to be grateful to the greasy-haired man for the second time that day.

"Well, that's nice." Lucy turned to his wife. "I always wanted to go to college, but my father thought it foolish when I should be married. It was good that I met Frank when I did. I might have run away down to college, myself."

"What a fantasy, Lucy. You did right as you did. Everyone knows that college weakens a woman's insides so that she can't have a baby. If you had gone to college, you wouldn't have had your precious Frank Jr., the male Milford who will oversee this property one day."

Lucy untied the ribbons of her bonnet, and lifted it carefully from her head and laid it to the side. "No. I wouldn't have had."

“There are places in life that a woman belongs.” Clara arranged her skirts. “At home, with family. Certainly not in a college.”

The air around his wife fairly crackled with energy. He put an arm around her shoulders and squeezed, so that she would calm down.

“Well, we will let you ladies rest.” Virgil set down his glass and importuned Mandy to do the same. “Will you dismiss school for the rest of the day Mr. Lakey? I think we all have business to do.”

“I will. Are you and Stew going back to the house?”

“I don’t want . . .”

“We are,” he stepped on his wife’s response. “Got lots to do.”

He helped Mandy up. Her body shook next to his. Oh, she was not pleased with him, but she needed to leave before she responded in a way to Clara Milford that would cause real trouble.

“Hope you get settled in to our town,” he spoke to the ladies. “You have a good day. We’re going home.”

They watched their steps carefully as he guided his wife away from her school to the center of Milford’s town square.

“How could you do that, Virgil?” Mandy charged at him.

“If you want to keep that school, you can’t play the hothead with that white lady. It won’t do no good.”

“She needs to know.”

“She was saying that stuff to get to you so she can get that house back. It’s no way to fight, and that woman . . . she don’t fight fair. I know. You want this done, Mandy, you going to have to do it my way.”

He stepped from her hot flesh to allow her to cool down and accept his words, as the real possibility they knew would happen one day.

The day they dreaded had come to pass at last.

CHAPTER FIVE

The rush of heatedness at Virgil's touch had nothing to do with the April day.

It's the baby.

But, she knew it wasn't the baby.

Dear Lord, how can I feel this way carrying a child inside of me? Help me.

Still, the firmness of his grip on her elbow, made her throat dry and her eyes moisten with sweat or tears. She didn't know which one.

"Where are you taking me?"

"Home." His deep voice firmed at her question, but she could tell he was surprised that she asked.

"What about March?"

"March is a child of the community. She will know there is no school and she'll be home when she wants."

Amanda knew that to be true, but still, she didn't want to rely so much on March's good sense to get herself home when the time came. She still was her mother.

"We could just let her know, husband."

His grip tightened a squeeze on her elbow and slid to her waist with a quickness.

Oh. For the days when he would hold her close like that, when they were newly married. What would she give for his regard for her like that again? "No. Better to get you home. You aren't feeling well."

Amanda stopped in her tracks in the town square, where they were just before his smithy. As much as she relished it, she shook loose from his hold.

"I'm just fine. You can get yourself on to work, and I'll take myself home if that's what you want."

Virgil's brow furrowed, and there was his thundercloud look. "Woman, I was not born yesterday. I'll take you home myself. I'll hitch up Pie right here and get you on the buckboard if you want. But you are going home."

Her uncle Isaac waved out to her from the smithy. She waved back, but refused to remove her own thundercloud look from her face.

"I'm the lead teacher of the school. I'll not be bullied by you or anyone else."

"Why do you have to be so stubborn about this?"

Her chest started heaving. She tried to stop it, but she couldn't. She squatted by some flowers and breathed deep to stop her chest from doing those things.

"I need you to understand."

"Understand what, Mandy?" He knelt by her in the red dirt and risked dirtying his beautiful broadcloth suit that fit him perfectly. He could be so lovely to her when he wanted.

"The school has to go on. It has to make it."

"I knows. I know. Why do you think I'm working like I do, going to the capital? It's all for you and the school. And March and Milford and the children. We ain't going anywhere as a people if we don't pull together and get education."

Her chest stopped heaving. He reached out and touched her arm, trying to help her up.

Isaac came running out from behind the anvil. He was bathed in sweat, but she couldn't stand the concern on his face. She didn't want him to think anything was seriously wrong with her, when it wasn't.

"You okay, Amanda?"

She reached out and touched her husband on the arm and he helped her up. "I'm fine. Virgil's looking out for me."

"Good. I'm glad that you made up then."

Virgil's head whipped over to fix her uncle with a stare. "We doing just fine. Lots of work left at the anvil from what I could see. Come on and help me hitch up my horses to take Mandy home."

"What're you talking about?"

But Virgil had already dragged him away, back to the smithy to get the horses. So unnecessary, but maybe he had a concern for the baby. She brushed the residual red dirt from her skirts and folded her hands to wait for him to come around the corner.

He tied the horses to a hitching post next to her and lifted her up onto the buckboard gently. "You need some lunch."

And some rest. She was a bit sleepy. "I got some leftover soup at home. I'll heat that up, and then I'll just take a rest."

His eyes seemed fixed on hers. “We can ask Pauline if she has any food. You look like you about to drop.”

She straightened herself up. “There’s no time for that. We’ve got to get to the county courthouse about those taxes and make sure those Milford women don’t ruin everything I’ve planned.”

For the first time, he put his eyes away from her and on the road. “It’s going to be okay.”

“They said something up in the capitol.”

“Well, we can’t worry about that. I said it will be okay and it will.”

She reached over and patted his thigh, all muscly and straining as he drove the horses over the buckboard. “I don’t doubt it will with you in charge, husband. And there’s no need to go to Pauline’s. I’ll be fine with the food that I have.”

He swiveled back to her. “I’ll trust you.”

The horses did an extra dance step to get closer to the house, just a little bit faster. Her heart’s ache eased. He must be happy about the baby. He just got tongue-tied about such things—that was all. He was happy. Why would he be so concerned about her getting to the house to rest?

She put a caressing hand to her belly again. “You can’t go causing so much trouble. I have stuff to do. Trying to make a future for you.”

The fluttering under her heart started again. Did the baby understand what she was talking about? She hoped so. It was just not fair for those women to come in, trying to stir things up. Mrs. Milford knew what she had meant when she had left the land and the house to them. Things might be a little shabby, a little questionable just now, but when Virgil came into his political position, once they all voted him in, it would all be fine. Nothing could happen, no protection, nothing could happen if it were not for protections written into the new constitution her husband had worked on.

He pulled up close to their front porch and hopped off the buckboard to make sure the horses were secure before he lifted her out of the wagon.

Her feet were flat on the ground but for a minute, when her husband swept her up in his arms, carrying her into the house amid her protests.

"Just making sure you safe, that's all."

Amanda ringed her arms around his neck. "Do you remember that after we got married, we would come to the house like this sometimes?"

"Mandy. Hush. There's no need of talking about that here at the noontime."

She whispered in his ear. "You only saying that because of the baby."

He shook his head and shifted her in his arms a bit. "Not true, Amanda."

"You never call me, Amanda." She laid her head on his shoulder. "You must remember those times too."

"And if I do?" Virgil lifted her up with another little heave when he reached the top of the stairs with her. "Nothing to do about it if you are to remain safe."

"But I am safe." She protested, and he laid her on the beautifully hewn pine bed he had made for Sally, but had brought her there instead.

"Good." He intoned. "I'm going back to the smithy."

"Don't leave just yet. I'm hungry."

"I'll get the soup for you, and then get back. Don't have no time to tarry with you today, Mandy."

His steps echoed with purpose as he stepped from the room and soon, Amanda smiled at the clattering of pans on the cook stove. She supposed he could heat up a pot of soup. Just for this one time.

Before she knew it, she had nodded off to sleep. She woke to see Virgil had brought forward an earthen bowl full of hot vegetable soup for her. She turned to him. "Thank you, husband. Did you make some for yourself? You have to get lunch before you go back to the smithy."

"I grabbed something out of the box. I'll be all right. I've got to go and be about town business."

Amanda sat herself up and drew the hot bowl of soup onto her lap. "Don't let me chase you off."

"I'm not. I just got business."

"I didn't mean to embarrass you about what I said just now."

She lifted the mug of soup to her lips and sipped the nourishing broth slowly, so she didn't bring it back up again. She lifted her lips a little bit to admit a piece of corn or two, but took it in very slowly.

"Wasn't embarrassed. I just don't think it's a good idea to be discussing that right now."

"That's fine. I apologize."

He sat there across from her, watching her take in the soup. "You go ahead. I'm not March. I'll be fine."

"Just making sure—is all."

She put the mug on the night table next to the bed. "That's all I can handle right now."

Virgil came to her side of the bed and unlaced her shoes, sliding them off her feet. "That should be better for now."

"It is. Feels much better. And my stockings too."

Her husband stood up and reached up, to where her fastenings were and unlaced the stockings from their anchors. Amanda shivered as his touch went higher under her skirts and tried not to think of the times he would touch her there—or even higher. *Dear Lord.*

She opened her eyes and he watched her with his stormy gaze. Facing that gaze and basking in the intensity of it, their eyes locked upon one another, and Amanda knew their minds were as one.

He was not going back to the smithy that afternoon.

Father God, why didn't he just go down to the smithy and let Amanda get her own soup? God knew Eve for a temptress. Mandy wasn't nothing but Eve's daughter.

Still, no use in blaming Mandy. Women had a weakness in their minds about emotional things, and it wasn't her fault at all.

It was his fault. This was no time to be lying around with his wife. Still, it had been since last year since he had been near her. He must have lost his mind. The orange scent in her hair and the smooth brown creaminess of her body was too much to take. Yes, she used to be all angular, but her face had now rounded, slowly filling for the coming of his child. He should have been able to resist.

The Lord knew him for a weak man.

He turned over to see she was staring back at him, with her long lashes blinking.

For this selfish moment that he took from her.

"Good morning," she said like the butter wouldn't melt in her mouth.

"It isn't morning, Mandy."

And his wife turned over on her back and stretched her arms out over her head. "I know."

He sat up in the bed, scrambling about for his clothes to dress himself.

"You looking like one of the barn cats after she had some cream."

"Hmmm. You mean one of the fat round ones who keep all the mice out there?"

He stopped scrambling, and Mandy laughed. "I don't care if you call me fat. I'm fine with it."

"Well, got plenty to do."

She sobered. "We both do. But there isn't a soul in Milford who begrudges this time you taking with me. At home."

The sucker punch in his gut didn't help his mind know any better that what she was saying was true. A man should cleave to his wife and keep her happy, especially as they were the examples in the community for everyone to look at.

Still.

"I can work on my sermon for tomorrow."

"That's a great idea. I can let Robert Lakey know you'll be preaching."

"What does he have to do with my preaching?"

"Well, he's been having words with people when you haven't been here."

He let his clothes slide to the floor. "What you say?"

"Well, he doesn't like to call it sermons, because he's not a minister touched by God as you have been, husband. He invites folk to the schoolhouse for words."

"What words?"

"He reads out of the Bible. It gives great comfort to the people."

"I just guess it does."

Mandy edged closer, touching him on his bare back. "It's nothing like what you do. Everyone has been wondering when you were coming. The words are too quiet. They want to hear some real preaching again. Been overdue for them."

No, there was no smiling at what she was saying. She wanted to know. Time to tell her. He took in a deep breath.

"After the Convention, some of the colored delegates stayed in Atlanta, talking about getting elected to the state house."

Now she sat up, and when she did, he could see the dimples appear back on her warm brown features. He let out a breath he didn't know he had been holding in. It would have been a different thing altogether to let the baby take her dimples away from him as well.

"And so what will happen?"

"There's going to be an election. I tried to talk to them about it, but the election's coming. I'll stand for the election, but it's going to be hard for us ones, because we don't know . . . well, some don't know if it is legal or not."

She pressed her warm body to his back. "It'll be for you. You weren't a slave before the war."

Her arms made a warmth around him, bolstering him, making him feel as if he could do anything. Just because Mandy said so. *Dear God. What was I before this woman, this light, came to me? I was nothing, I had nothing. Thank you.*

"They were talking. This is why I was late. Saying that they were going to throw us out if we got elected."

She sat back from him and the cold came in on him. "Who said?"

"The Democrats."

"Well, they should just try it. What do they mean throwing people out of duly elected offices? They didn't write the Constitution."

"Well, they kind of did. We just wrote the new Constitution down. The government in Washington said it's okay, and Georgia is back in the Union, and there's an election. But it might not be legal, they been saying."

He turned around and watched her mind spinning, doing cartwheels like March did in the red Georgia clay. Her braids made a curtain all around her, shielding all of her beauty from him.

Good thing too. They didn't need to be up in here into the night. And he really did need to work on his sermon for tomorrow.

"The election will happen. It will be legal. We're going to pray on this, starting tomorrow. If the people in Milford and Crumpton send you, they cannot repudiate you. What was the war about? What did President Lincoln say?"

"Honey, he's been gone from us three years now. He can't say a word. It's Johnson."

"I don't want to talk about that man. He's terrible."

Virgil agreed. Still, Johnson was the president. "Johnson's putting things back like in the old times."

She slumped forward in his arms. "To make everyone slaves again? I can't believe it."

"He's given the land back to the owners. No doubt, the Milford ladies would find a friend in him. Still, if it ever came to that, you, me and March be the first ones gone, I'm promising you that."

"And the baby."

"Of course, Mandy. The baby too."

"Why didn't you say the baby then?"

'Cause there is no baby. He wanted to curse himself. Pulling her back, he looked into her eyes. "I just didn't, is all."

"You don't love the baby."

"Mandy. This is foolishness. I love you. You knows that."

She put a hand to her rounded stomach. "I do, but I want you to love the baby."

"It's mine, and I'll take care of it."

"You don't see God and you love him."

Lord Almighty, this woman could get him tied up in more knots than what he could know. "Of course. A baby is different."

"A baby? Our baby is a gift from God. How can you deny love for it?"

He stood up and gathered up his clothes. "I'm not getting into this with you now. I have to get my sermon done, and I got to be in the right mood for it. I told you what you've been after me to know. Now let me be."

He began to get dressed in a hurry. Lord, he and his wife up in here rolling around with one another, and who knows what March was getting into. If the day hadn't been so hot in April, he would have warmed at his neglect of his child. A pastor, mayor and constitutional delegate, he had to take the responsibility in these affairs, no matter what education Mandy had. He had to show control. And he failed.

Miserably. He leaned over, kissed her on the forehead and strode out of the room, folding back his cuffs as he went out, dressed more informally to check on his livestock.

Lord knew it didn't do to show a woman you loved her too much. It would become a contest of how low she could bring him down, and Mandy had her way enough ever since he got back. If he lost sight of what was important, she wouldn't have his protection anymore, and in these hard times, there was much to do to protect and keep close the people you loved.

Because if Andrew Johnson had his way, they would all be back in chains.

He would fight to the last drop in his body to see that he and his family would never be enslaved again.

CHAPTER SIX

"You feeling okay?"

When Amanda came through the door of the church service the next morning, Pauline was on her. She brought March down with her to help her set up. Now at Pauline's mention, though . . .

"I could use a little help. Thank you." She sat down and watched as Pauline took over setting up the sanctuary in the brand new church building Virgil and his crew finished about eighteen months ago, after he had burned down the old one. Placed right in the middle of town on the furthest edge of the town square, her husband had said he wanted folk from land and sea to know that Milford, Georgia served God.

Thinking about Virgil set up a chill in her again, and she wrapped her shawl around her. These feelings made no sense. First, she was extremely hot, and then she would be cold and need her shawl. The baby in her seemed not to know what it wanted, going back and forth.

It will be all right, baby. It's going to be fine.

She wanted to sing a little song, croon the baby to comfort, but she was afraid someone would tell Virgil she was talking to herself or worse, to the spirits, so she hummed a spiritual they liked to sing around here, "Ev'ry time I feel the Spirit." It was an appropriate song to sing, because every time she felt the baby move in her, she wanted to pray in gratitude. Just as the song said.

March ran up to her sitting in the back row, and Pauline followed close behind. "May I play some more?"

"You going to get your church dress dirty." Pauline frowned.

"She will." Amanda overruled her friend. "It's all right, though. The Lord loves dirt too."

"Yay." March lifted up her arms and ran into the outdoors, skipping and waving her arms over her head.

They locked gazes and both burst into laughter. "That child is something else." Pauline intoned.

"She sure is."

"She been worried about you."

She twisted the shawl ends in her hand. "Really?"

"Yes. Coming down asking me to look in on you while Virgil away. Now she come to me saying something more now that he's home. He giving you a hard time?"

She ignored the heaves in her chest. "More like he giving me nothing at all."

Pauline held her by her hand. "You don't fret about that. Look, with some men, they can't see the baby, they don't know it, it's not real to them until it comes."

"It's not that. He just . . ." She took in a deep shuddering breath that rattled through her lungs. "He didn't want a baby."

Pauline balled up her fists like she was about to go into battle. Amanda wanted to smile, but from Pauline's narrowed eyes, she could see her friend was in no mood to be trifled with. "I saw him when he came home, and I told him not to bother you with that foolishness."

"Well, he can't help it. It's all in him. It's like he's mad at me or something."

"And you didn't get this way alone."

"Exactly. I don't know what to say to him about it. To make it better."

"Go on ahead and do what you got to do. Long as he still being nice to you. When it comes, I'll be there for you, but I got to say, you looking peaked. Even with your pretty brown skin. You need to let Mr. Lakey put them classes together and rest."

"I can teach sitting down."

"You ain't heard what I said, did you? "

"Yes, ma'am." Her voice came meekly, but a small laugh bubbled in her, and she couldn't help but let it out. Pauline gave a little laugh too, but her countenance was serious.

"I'ma talk to him about making a bed ties for you next to the kitchen in your house. Maybe one at the school too."

"Mr. Lakey is there. And now these two Milford daughters." She tied the shawl before her. Then untied it.

"Yeah. I seen them two. Old devil Clara acting like she own the place. Lucy always been all right with me, but Clara. She need a proper distraction to get right with the Lord."

She let go of her shawl ends. "I'll thank you to remember we are in the Lord's house, Pauline Baxter."

Pauline shook her head and the designs in her Sunday headwrap danced. “I’ll say what’s needed. He knows that.”

“Well. They probably got the money to pay the taxes, and we’ll lose the house.”

“Who said that?”

“I don’t know. I just assumed.”

“Them two is back trying to get the house because they don’t have money. I’m sniffing around. Where are Clara’s girls? She say that they in some fancy school somewhere, but I don’t know. Take money to keep them there. I’m looking at their gowns. They not new this year, maybe last year. Didn’t you see?”

She shook her head, shamefaced. The gowns were newer than hers were—that’s all she could tell.

“It’s the baby. Yeah, babies have a way of making themselves the center of the world. You didn’t notice.”

“I’m still worried.”

“We need to find out what they have. And that doesn’t mean you all can’t get the money in on time for the tax year.” Pauline patted her hand.

The heaves in her chest went away. “I’m glad to hear that.” She loosened the ribbons on her bonnet and edged it off, trying to ignore the thin rim of sweat in it. She patted her bun of braids to get them to smooth down.

“Good. I’m taking your man to the side to let him know you need to rest.”

Some of the Baxters began to enter the vestibule, so Pauline tossed out, “It’s going to be all fine. We asking for the Lord’s blessing today.” Pauline straightened out her short body and hugged her before she started to go off.

As if on cue, her husband stepped through the door and came to her through the aisle. He must be disturbed to come in and step in the aisle of the Lord before church even began. Maybe this was his way of making up to her.

"Virgil," Pauline straightened herself. "Praise God, how are you?"

"Praise God, how you, Pauline?"

"Blessed in spirit, as are you. As are you." Pauline was the only one in Milford proper who could make her strong husband cower, just a little bit. Well, except for her. She could see Virgil seemed distracted in maintaining that preacher pride in himself. Because Pauline knew. Everything.

"Come to see to my wife." Virgil sat down next to her.

"About time." Pauline edged herself away from the bench. "I'm going to find my man. You, Mandy, you need to sit back here today in case you get sick." Pauline eyed Virgil. "Not up front where you are used to sitting. Too far from the privy."

"I understand."

"We'll sit next to you, once I find Isaac."

"Thank you, Pauline."

The words he spoke to her were the first since they had been together yesterday morning. He said, "Can I get you anything?"

"No. I'll be fine."

He stood up. "I'm sure Pauline will help you."

"Not you, because you will be busy."

Virgil sat back down. "I'm thanking you to remember that I'm doing my job and I need to have the peace of the Lord around me this morning."

"You should have thought of that yesterday."

"We'll discuss this at home, wife."

"As you wish."

"It is my wish, Amanda." When he called her by her full first name, it was over. Really over.

Tears smarted in the corners of her eyes, and she used the edge of the shawl to get at them as she watched him walk away to the front of the church with a straight proud carriage. In her heart, she was glad of today. It was not "words" with Robert Lakey, but a rousing Sunday service because everyone was glad that Virgil, as her minister, was back. Praise the Lord indeed.

He was back in body, but what about his spirit? His mind? Had all her ideas to get him into politics been wrong? Maybe it was better for him to be here at home, with his people, petitioning for help to other politicians.

She knew though, no other man in the near vicinity had the pull, attraction, charisma, or common sense he did. Many sacrifices had to be made these difficult days. A sacrifice of the few for the many.

Tilting herself back on the bench, she leaned back, rubbing her front for comfort and wondered. What sacrifice did she have to make for him?

He chose to talk about the sacrifice Abraham made of his one and only son, Isaac. Then, maybe his parishioners would understand what had to be done. There would be an election, but there would be questions about it. Did Mandy understand? She seemed excited about the election and hopeful for the future. Still, could it be said she truly understood the legality of the election was a question, or did she just say the things she said because of the baby?

"So when God asks us to lay up our treasure, we got to do it. Can't just keep it for ourselves. These are gifts God Almighty has asked for us to do. We cannot hesitate."

"Amen!" Pauline shouted, always his loudest parishioner and when the preaching got good to her, she didn't hesitate. He hoped she was truly enjoying it, not preparing herself to get him into a corner somewhere and tell him about he wasn't living up to some high standard.

"We all have mighty crosses to bear. And soon, I gots to take up mine again. Gotta go back to Atlanta for a time."

His crowd of parishioners groaned together, and Pauline put her shouting hand down. Her hands stilled.

Dear God. Be with me as I pray.

"These are times of hope and change. We going to be voting soon."

"Yes, Lord! Voting time has come!" Now Calla, Pauline's sister-in-law, was on it.

"Indeed." He stood a little straighter and gripped the sides of the pulpit. "There's several of us going there. We going to be part of the Georgia Legislature. Finally, we going to have a chance to talk, to have our say, to be part of the world!"

"Amen, amen and amen!" Pauline waved her hands. Good.

"I have work to do elsewhere, but I know Milford will be fine. It will be in capable hands. My wife."

The energy of the church shifted from him to Amanda, sitting in the back row of the church, looking as green as a woman with shining brown skin could look. "My treasure," he continued, "she'll be here taking care. Running things like she always does."

His church fell silent.

Help me with my words Lord.

"Lord will provide for her, amen. He going to see her through. We got to have faith that Amanda Smithson, cloaked in the blessings of the blood of Jesus, is going to handle whatever God lays before her."

Calla gave out a weak "Amen," but Pauline sat there, lips pursed, hands folding. Saying nothing.

"Abraham didn't know. He didn't know what would be required of him. All he knew, praise God, was that he had to do what God wanted him to do. And if that meant lifting up that knife, and sinking it deep into the chest of his child, then he had to do what God would want him to do. Anyone, anyone of us who believes in the Word of the Lord knows this is all we can do."

Was Mandy's beautiful face bathed in tears? Or sweat? He couldn't see her from the back of the church. He gripped the podium, feeling sorrow she had to sit so far from him, in case she got sick.

I never realized before how much I leaned on her.

Their connection was greater than he had with Sally. This woman, Mandy, was the rock God had provided to build his ministry upon. What a blessing she was. What a treasure. *I love her so much. What would I do? What could I be without her?*

He didn't want to find out.

"Pray. Pray for understanding in this time of sacrifice." He stepped out from behind the pulpit and into the blessed aisle. He had to see her for himself.

No, she wasn't crying. She was sweating, a whole lot of sweat, like Sally was when she gave birth to that white man's child, who ripped her apart and ripped her from life. Before he knew it, he was beside her and caught her in his arms, just as she slumped over.

Pauline stood on her feet instantly as if she had just been aware of Amanda's passing out, but he knew.

Please Jesus.

He loosened her collar from around her neck and leaned in to listen to her heart and lungs. She was still breathing, praise Him.

"Mandy, honey. Mandy. Wake up."

And just when he thought things couldn't be worse, and nothing could happen anymore, Amanda's body went rigid in his arms. Calling her name over and over, his heart sank. She would not answer him.

He knew nothing else. Pauline came forward with some water from the pump, looking very grave.

"Mind has done seized up."

"Help her!" He roared. "God no, Please no, not again!"

What had he done? What could he do? How could he help her? The very thing he had feared when he held her in his arms not two full days ago was happening. Amanda was dying in his arms and he was powerless again, to stop it. Just like Sally.

"Bring her on up to the house," Pauline directed, not sounding any different than the sergeants in the fields during the Big War.

His arms, he could use them to carry her, but his arms, they made a terrible place for a woman to be. A terrible place for a woman to die.

God save my wife. Please. Save her.

Her body, rigid and stick straight did not bend, but Virgil picked her up and followed Pauline out of the door with his treasure cradled in his arms, careful of her head and feet.

Just as he reached the doorway of Pauline's cabin, Mandy's body relaxed in his arms and she breathed harder.

"The dead man's fix." Pauline intoned, "Put her on the bed."

"What's wrong with her?" He laid her down gently, took a handkerchief out of his pocket, and began to wipe the terrifying amount of sweat from Amanda's brow. "Is she going to die?"

"Virgil. You got to be strong for her now. You stay right there with her and get to praying. I don't want, don't need to hear no weak words from you. Everything got to be strong for her. You got that?" Pauline's gaze locked on his eyes and held tight.

Calla came bustling into the cabin with a load of linens in her arms. He looked up at her with questioning eyes. "What's all that for?"

The burning coal fire went out of Pauline's eyes. "Dead man's slump is a seizure. Mind is saying to the body, can't hold on to the baby. The baby is poison in her. It has to go."

His mind raced around, not at all being as strong as Pauline had directed him to be. "Amanda."

Calla brought the linens forward, shaking her head at his wife's prone posture. "She be losing it for sure."

Virgil turned and looked at his wife, who was breathing more like normal and noticed the beautiful curve of her lips. He did the only thing he knew how to do.

Dear God. If this child be poison, evidence of my sin and passion from this woman, remove it. But please, Father God, please, don't take my Mandy. I'm not strong like Abraham. I can't, I can't lose that sacrifice. If you take her from me, I won't be able to stand and do the work that you have me to do to help all of your children be free. Please. Help me now.

Just like that, her eyes flew open and fixed themselves on him.

Thank you, God.

But before she could part her beautiful lips to utter a single word to him, her luscious mouth became a great gaping hole and Mandy gripped at herself and screamed. He backed away at the rapid change in her, afraid for the pain that she was experiencing.

Calla pulled at him. "You need to get on away while we take care of this."

"I ain't going anywhere. You hear me?" He stood and pulled off his broadcloth coat.

"Virgil. This is women's business. You got to go." Calla insisted.

Pauline turned from a concoction she was making. "Leave him be. He seen Sally in all of her wrestling with the Angel of Death. Ain't nothing different. He be all right." She stepped to his wife and lifted Amanda's skirts and felt around, causing Amanda to cry out again, the familiar cries of a woman's agony ringing through his ears yet another time.

He rolled up his shirtsleeves, kneeling next to his wife. Gently, he grasped her hands in his and knew his face was bathed in tears, not sweat. He did not care.

If there was some wrestling to do to God to save his wife, he wanted to be ready to face whatever was going to come their way. They would face the Angel of Death together. And dare him to win this time.

CHAPTER SEVEN

Well, Virgil had gotten his wish, she supposed. And that's what mattered, didn't it? That her husband got what he wanted. No matter the sacrifice on her part.

Still, she had to get back up. Get going. They wanted that tax money for the school by the start of July, and there was still no way, no known way they could get it.

"Get back in that bed." Pauline frowned at her attempts to get dressed for the school.

"It's Wednesday. I've lain around enough. Two days is enough for the children to be out. They need to learn more."

"What did I tell you?" Pauline's short frame barely cast a shadow over her, but her friend stood firm in front of her, fists on her hips.

All of sudden, Amanda sobbed. "I want to go home. I don't want to take up the bed that rightfully belongs to you and your husband."

"No one to do for you there."

"What do you mean?"

Pauline nudged her down with a tap on the shoulder. "Virgil had to go to Atlanta."

She must have been run down by a horse, since she fell back on the bed so quickly. "What're you saying?"

"He ain't here. I'm taking care of you. You can't do for yourself and March just now. Maybe tomorrow."

"Why isn't he here?"

"He said he told you about why he had to go back so quick."

The tears poured like a spring freshwater gush into her ears as she cast about in her mind for something Virgil said to her. "No. I mean, I don't. I can't remember."

"You need a little more time to get into your head."

She sprang back up. "What about school? I've got to get back for the children."

The wetness on the front of her nightgown stopped her, and she touched her breasts, her own body a foreign creature to her. "What's happening to me?"

A look came onto Pauline's face that Amanda had never seen before. Sadness? Fear? She turned from Amanda, reached into a trunk, and brought her a length of mean, hard cloth and a fresh nightgown. "Got to bind up your breasts, honey. They weeping milk because they think there's a baby here. You wrap them in this, they'll stop."

Amanda touched the rough hard cloth and cringed. "I don't want that on me."

"Can't be helped. I'll show you."

There was no time for modesty as Amanda pulled the drenched white nightgown from her body and put it to the side. Pauline pushed the gown to the wooden floor; it made a whapping sound from the wetness, and a heady sweet scent of milk came up from it and hit them full bore in the face.

Amanda stared into her friend's knowledgeable face, and as Pauline opened the length of cloth and began to wrap it around her body; she shivered to see her usual stalwart friend crying too. "I don't want that on me."

Pauline was much stronger than her, and in short order, she was mummified inside the hateful cloth. She donned the fresh nightgown and laid back into the bed.

"It'll stop by morning. Your body just got to understand there ain't no baby. That's all. I'll get you some breakfast. I sent March up to your house to gather eggs, so you can have cooked ones to build you back up again."

The fact that they were going to waste the rarity of eggs on her was enough to sober her. *I've got to get better. There are children here who need me.*

"Thank you. I'm sorry to be such trouble. I really should be able to go back home soon."

Pauline squeezed her hand. "Tomorrow. You be feeling much better." Her head dipped down. "Happened to me 'bout four times. And it's harder when it get to this point. But by the third day, you be feeling better."

The blood in Amanda's veins froze. She had forgotten about Pauline's difficulties in having a baby. "Four times? Like this?"

She shook her head. "This was back in the bad times, so I didn't have no Pauline to come and care for me. I had to get back up and get back in the fields next day, so I know you be fine. I think that's what might not have helped me get strong, 'cause I always having to get back to work. Think it hurt my insides."

Amanda's own insides quaked at the heartfelt confession by this woman who had come to mean so much to her. To be the kind of mother she had never known. And Pauline had even known her mother. "I'm so sorry," she whispered.

"It's not happening like that for you. You get rest. You want to go back to school, so Isaac's making you something special to help you. But listen. I don't want you feeling sorry about yourself. That's why you only get three days."

She nodded at her admonition. "It would be easier if Virgil was here."

Pauline waved a hand in the air like something bad had invaded her small cabin. "He wasn't doing nothing but getting in me and Calla's way. He say he had to go to Atlanta, I say, go. Get out of here. You driving me crazy."

Amanda looked up at her. "Really?"

"He thinking you going to die. Like Sally."

Her heart squeezed tight in her chest at the thought that her husband had to relive one of the worst days in life all over again. "He must have been so sad."

"He was out of his mind. I had to take him to the side and put him on his horse myself."

She couldn't help but chuckle at the thought of small, squat Pauline putting her large, muscular husband on Pie's back to go to Atlanta.

"I hope you not holding it against him. He's a man. You wanted him to go and do these politic things, you know."

"If he hadn't, someone over in Crumpton—probably a Democrat, would be representing this area." Amanda spoke rapidly. “It was the only way. He’s the only choice.”

“Really now?” Pauline went to her cook stove and brought her back some broth and bread.

In that second, her loss went from her mind. It reminded her that she would heal. Eventually.

My poor baby. Her heart lurched. “Guess I’ll always be March’s mother.”

“That’s for true. And others.”

She tore off a chuck of bread and chewed on it, trying to nourish herself for the hard road of work ahead. “The others. They didn’t stay inside of you.”

“Told you. I think I never got a chance to heal up right. We making sure you going to be healed up right. Virgil be needing another son to help him to . . .”

Pauline put a hand to her mouth.

“Another son?” She stopped chewing and the wad of bread stuck in her throat, turning into a stopper.

Her friend took her hand off of her mouth and took the bread from her hand, putting it on the tray and a little of the broth slopped out onto the bed sheet and quilt.

“It were a little boy child.”

She had carried a boy. The boy child everyone said she ought to be giving Virgil—so he could raise up sons to help care for the Milford town and church. She had almost been successful. But something went wrong. How hard it was, not knowing what was wrong, why the baby wouldn’t stay inside of her, to ever imagine doing it again.

“Where is he?”

“Oh honey, Virgil took care of it. Built a little coffin and put him down where all the Baxters are.”

"Did he give him a name?"

"A name? No child. He didn't."

She dipped her spoon into the dark brown liquid and ate of the tepid liquid, willing the moisture to soften the lump in her throat to nourish her.

If he had blessed the little baby as a child of God and put their son into the cold ground, why no name? Did he care so little?

She couldn't ask that of Pauline. That was question for her husband, when he returned.

Staring straight ahead at the beautiful ringed pattern on Pauline's quilt, she spoke aloud to herself. "His name will be Lawrence. Lawrence Virgil Smithson."

She dipped the spoon in again and again until the liquid was half-gone. Then, carefully so she didn't dirty Pauline's clean floor, she set the mug on the floor next to the bed, turned over and sobbed until she ran out of tears.

Coming to Atlanta this time, reminded him what he never remembered—he and Mandy had never traveled together. He had gone up to Oberlin to bring her back home when she had run off, but that was nearly two years ago and not a trip together.

He had not done the simple courtesy to his wife of giving her a honeymoon trip.

Thinking of that made him want to turn Pie right back around and bring her here.

But Atlanta? Such a noisy and dirty place. He did not like the rough loudness or how boisterous and forward it was. It was the place where, in all likelihood, they would be living.

When he had traveled around before the Civil War, he had seen big cities before, but this one was a big city in the making. No, he would want to take his wife at least to Charleston or Buford. Some coastal city. Not here. Clearly, here was for business, it was about meetings for constitutional conventions and voting and building a new state capital—if the voters approved of it in the upcoming election.

It was better for it to be here than in poor sad Milledgeville when he had capitol business before for Mrs. Milford, to bring the papers certifying him as Mayor of Milford. Now, this was different.

He pulled Pie up to his boarding house on Broad Street. This was where he had stayed during the Constitutional Convention. He wanted to lodge in a place that wouldn't give him a hard time for being Negro and had a Christian boarding house owner. He had succeeded in one, but not quite the other. Unfortunately.

He recognized the tall, broad-shaped Negro man about his age waving to him. He waved back as he anchored Pie to the hitching post.

"Hello, Smithson. We was about to send some folk out after you."

"Things happened at home. Made it hard to get away." Vigil greeted his friend and fellow pastor, Henry McNeal Turner.

"Sorry to hear. It's going be all right, though?"

"Eventually." Virgil's lips grew tighter, not really wanting to talk about it all, but Henry kept pushing.

"Let's pray."

Out there in the street, Henry put an arm around his shoulders and intoned. "Dear God, help this man though his time of travail and struggle. You know we have a mighty work to do here, and we need all folks on board to help us come through this. Stay with him and stay by our side. In Jesus' name."

Amen. The men lifted their heads. "You better be moving to Atlanta, you know."

Virgil shook his head and took up his grip. "I'm the Mayor of Milford too."

"Election Day is coming up fast. 'Bout two weeks. Your town ready?"

"They'll be ready."

"Good. We want no funny business about anything. You go home this time and let the people know."

"Thanks, Henry."

Henry clapped him on the shoulder and followed him into the boarding house. "You ought to turn that poky little one-horse town over to someone else."

"Wouldn't be here without Milford. And my wife has the school there. The school has to get where it needs to be."

"Bless Mrs. Smithson. I like to meet her sometime. Sound like someone I should know. There's schools here too we are trying to get going. Might get her involved with one of them."

Virgil shook his head and stepped into the parlor to arrange for his lodging. "I don't know if that will sit too well with her. These people are her family, she isn't likely to abandon them."

"Well now, are they her family, or are you?"

Truth to tell, Virgil wasn't sure anymore. The sounds of Mandy's screams at her pain echoed through his ears and made him want to cringe. Her rounded body divesting itself of that boy baby, the long skinny boy Pauline had thrust at him to bury in the graveyard, haunted him. Taunted him.

"Hard to tell sometimes."

Henry laughed and rang the bell again for Mrs. Paine, the owner of the boarding house to come forward to register him. "Wives can be a funny thing sometimes. Hard to tell what they want and don't want. Been married to Mrs. Turner for ten years, and I still don't know."

Virgil grimaced as Mrs. Paine came into sight, matching his grimace. Mandy wasn't like that necessarily, but she was kind of hard to explain to people if they didn't know her. His wife was a one-of-a-kind woman.

"Sorry, Mr. Smithson. No rooms just now. Should have kept the room. You can go down the street to the Fortune's, there be something there I think."

"Should have kept the room?" Virgil repeated. "Why would I do that? I knew I was going away."

"I've got arrangements with certain clients, Mr. Smithson. You been a good steady customer over these past five months. I might have done something."

Something like rent out his paid-for room while he was gone? He had seen that happen before. And he didn't miss Mrs. Paine's appraisal of him. Shameless. Professing her Christian beliefs, but he didn't miss the way she looked at him. She had at least fifteen to twenty years on him and didn't seem to respect his marriage. Not a very Christian manner to behave in.

"I'll get something elsewhere. Thank you." Virgil turned from her and went back out into the humid Atlanta air, looking up and down the streets. What could he possibly do now?

"You ain't going to be here long this time. I think it's time you come and visit me and Mrs. Turner."

"I don't want to impose." He imagined dumping a friend on Amanda at this time when she was trying to heal and didn't wish to think of the consequences.

"Not a problem. Come on with me. We can talk there better anyway. See? This is what I'm saying. You all need to move here."

He tied his horse behind Turner's carriage and climbed in with him so that they could talk on the way to his home. When they arrived there, it was clear Henry had done well for himself to afford to live in a nice-sized house. "Lots of us living here in these boarding houses over here. Tunis lives down the street. We all getting ready for the session come fall."

"I see." The nicely built houses of brick rebuilt after Sherman had marched through, and a comfortable place for Negroes to be able to live in a neighborhood together—all working together for a common goal—it was very appealing. Could he persuade Mandy of the benefits of dirty, noisy Atlanta?

"There's my school over there. Got Atlanta College started there already. Going to start up Morris right next to it. Share resources and grow up together. A new seminary is down from that. A whole area of Negroes being educated for different ends, all together, here in Atlanta. And it's not too far from the City Hall where we'll be meeting until there's a capitol."

He and Henry took care of the horses and stabled them. His point was well made. People were bound to choose an up-and-coming city to go to school in. Henry pointed out nice grounds with brick buildings being built. Maybe this was the answer.

This could be the way Amanda wouldn't have to worry about no tax money lining the pockets of those fools in Crumpton. They wanted the money from them, or they wanted them out.

A dawn brightened Virgil's heart. This would be the way. The tax collector in Crumpton would get nothing, and Amanda would still get what she wanted. A school to educate teachers and preachers. They were doing it already right here in Atlanta.

When they came around to the house, a golden brown woman wearing a modest white cap and white apron over a rich dark brown dress stood on the porch. "What are you doing here in the middle of the day, Henry?"

"Oh, Mother. Thought to bring you some company home."

"Well, Tunis beat you here." She pointed a wooden spoon over to the gentleman sitting on the porch. "He's always here looking for something to eat."

"Hey, didn't see you over there, Tunis! You remember Tunis Campbell from the session, Virgil."

"I do." He stepped forward to shake the man's hand. Tunis Campbell, with silken black hair and a mischievous smile, was the kind of gentleman who made himself known. And apparently at Turner's table.

"This is Virgil Smithson, Mother."

He shook hands with the handsome Mrs. Turner.

"He staying with us for a bit?"

"No room at the inn, Mother. You have it." Henry laughed at his joke a bit and his wife smiled. "Always room for one more. You and Tunis can share the guest room."

Better than sleeping in the barn, although he had slept in many of them in his day. "I would appreciate it, ma'am."

"Mighty welcome. I'm going in to dish up some lunch. Glad you could make it."

He was too. *I'm meant to see this side of things. This is what Mandy and I could have.*

"No wife this time?" Tunis stood to greet him more directly after Mrs. Turner went into the house.

"She's incapacitated." How good it was to use a long word that fit just right. Sometimes his education fell short of other men like these.

"You didn't say that, Smithson. Sorry to hear."

"Anything we can do?" Tunis put in, genuinely concerned.

"She just had a baby. That's all."

"Lord a' mercy, you sure are close-mouthed, Smithson. Congrats." Henry clapped him on the back another time.

"She lost the baby. So she's getting better back home."

"Sorry to hear that." Tunis shook his head.

Henry nodded. "Mrs. Turner lost three in between our two. Wasn't easy. We have to thank God for the life that he gives us. It's all so precious. So fragile."

"Amen." Tunis agreed. "We've never had that happen, but it must be hard."

"Yes."

"God will bless you. There'll be more. Got two fine boys." Henry said. "You'll see. Come on in, you two. Make yourselves at home."

"If God wills it." Tunis gestured to Virgil to enter the Turner home before he did. Kind of him.

"Yes, indeed." It had to be God's will. Not his. Not Mandy's. That's the powerful lesson to be learned this time around. He had no say in these things. They needed to stay and wait upon the Lord.

CHAPTER EIGHT

It had been nice of Robert to push her in the chair Isaac made for her into the sun. It felt much better being outside than inside, letting the spring warmth soak into her bones. Apparently, Virgil had issued some kind of edict about not letting school go back into session until he returned, but the children still congregated in front of the Milford house to play. Since she and March were staying at Pauline and Isaac's house closer to the town square, it was easier to come down here.

But she was bored.

"If either of you have any mending to do, I can help." Amanda offered.

"Oh, little Franklin kicks holes in his dresses something fierce." Lucy offered. "If you could help, that would be great."

"I would be happy to." She smiled at her, purposefully not looking in Clara's direction.

Lucy brought everything to her that she needed: needles, thread, dresses. Picking up the dresses and examining the holes, it was clear to Amanda that

Franklin's way of rebelling against wearing the dress was to kick holes in them. If he had some small knickerbockers . . . Still, some women could be funny about stopping their boys from wearing dresses. If she had a boy, and he were Franklin's age, she would put him in short pants.

But I do have a boy. He's lying over there in the cold ground. No one brought him to me so that I could say goodbye to him. Little Lawrence, who didn't have a chance to draw breath on this earth.

She busied herself working over the pile of white dresses. She could not allow herself to be buried in worrying. There was too much to do for the babies who were here already. The court date was coming up in a few days, and she still puzzled about how to get the money to make sure the house remained secure.

"Let them have the house. I'll build another schoolhouse for you." Her husband's deep tones resonated throughout her mind as she remembered what he had said when they worried about if the family would come back and claim the house from them.

But that wouldn't do. This was Milford College now, not just some schoolroom. They were educating the youngest ones for a purpose, not just to read and write for fieldwork. The six older ones were being made ready to be in the classroom or the pulpit someday. This was something more.

She knew Virgil was hurt when her silence meant she wasn't keen on a schoolhouse built by him but wanted the large white, slightly ramshackle Milford farmhouse changed up. No, it wasn't outfitted for a school, but they would get it there. With help and money.

Of which there was too little of both.

"A lady should stay in bed at such a delicate time. You aren't fit to be seen, after all."

What was Clara jabbering on about now?

"Women should not be seen when they are expecting a happy arrival. I never went outside. And don't wash your your hair. It's not good for the baby."

"Clara," Lucy's head was bent over some embroidery. "Where did you get those ideas?"

"It's how things were done in Tennessee. I learned a lot of things at my mother's knee. Since I grew up with one. Really. Some people who don't have mothers grow up perfectly wild. It's good our children have us, Lucy."

"They're a precious gift. May others be richly blessed by that gift from God."

The silence fell and instead of listening to Clara's hateful ways of putting Amanda down, her ears picked up the loud belching sound of the train sounding in the distance, slowing down. Could it be Virgil?

Please Lord, let it be my husband. She ached for him so. How hateful it was that he had to be away on political business just now, but she hoped he would be back soon. Then she could say how sorry she was for everything, the baby and all, and they could start all over again.

Then she remembered he had taken Pie, so he would probably be arriving back home on horseback. Who was the train stopping for?

"A visitor." Lucy whispered.

"Or a delivery." Clara put down her own needlework. "Something new." She spread her skirts and sighed. *Serves her right.* Let her suffer along with the rest of us at the shortage of cloth, fabric and money.

Robert stopped reading his book. "Stopping too long for a delivery. Might be a visitor." He marked his page and stepped off the porch, stretching as he went. "I better go see who it is."

She wanted to say from her perch just off Mrs. Milford's porch, that greeting visitors was a job for the mayor—her husband. She could do it in his stead, but it felt so good to be in the chair working on little baby dresses. Even if little Franklin was not her baby. Her contribution was real, and it was the right thing to do. Bending her head to her work, she paid no mind, until she lifted her head up to rub a crick from her neck.

A tall blond man accompanied Robert, and they were talking in a very congenial sort of way. Of course, Robert made friends with everyone, except for Virgil, so there was no telling.

"Good afternoon."

"It's still the morning time, I believe, sir. Whose company do we have here?" Clara demurred.

Amanda wanted to roll her eyes. Now that the company was brought to her, she stood on halting legs, as when Pie had her baby pony Cookie, and went to the gentleman. She did not extend her hand, but rather kept a fold of her dress in her hand to prevent herself from shaking hands with a stranger. Remembering how Virgil had acted about Robert, a known friend, shaking hands with a stranger would not make Virgil happy.

"Welcome to Milford, sir. May we have the honor of your acquaintance?"

Robert spoke up in his puppy dog way. "This is Jack Kirchner. He was in the Union Army from Pennsylvania."

Clara shifted back into her chair. "Heavens, we're being invaded from all sides."

Amanda cut her a sideways glance. How rude of her. But Jack Kirchner laughed. "'Fraid that's not my problem, ma'am. Blame the Federal Government. They want to make sure you're doing right down here. I'm from thc Freedman's Bureau."

"Really?" Amanda twisted the dress in her hands a bit. "I read that you were disbanded."

"Not officially. Not yet. Still have a few more months to go. I volunteered to come to some of the most set back places, as Milford is. To see if I could give a hand."

"A hand in what, pray?" Clara's voice rose and her blue-black curls bounced around. "We're just fine here. Certainly not in the need of help from the Freedman's Bureau."

Jack shook his head regarding her. "I beg to differ, ma'am. You Georgians, well, you haven't been as nice as you might to the freed folk. They're in need of a little more help than you've been willing to give."

"I'll thank you, sir." Clara stood. "I'm a proud daughter of Tennessee."

"Oh. I apologize."

"There's quite a difference you know. A large difference."

"Of course, ma'am."

Mandy wanted to laugh, as she hadn't in days, at seeing someone tell Clara how to be. *Dear God, please help me.* Gathering her composure, barely, she stepped forward again. "Well, what kind of help are you looking to provide, Mr. Kirchner?"

"You must be Amanda Stewart. I've heard much about you."

"Smithson. Amanda Smithson. I'm married to the mayor here, Virgil Smithson."

"That explains a lot about the school then. If you married, you must not be teaching."

"No sir. I still teach. Myself and Mr. Lakey. Whom you've met here."

Jack regarded Robert again. "There have not been many reports to the AMA lately."

Amanda lowered her head. "We've had some fiscal problems in maintaining the school. Sometimes there are other emergencies required to keep things going. No real time to file reports."

"We're going to get that straightened out, though." Robert jumped in.

"Well, that's why I'm here. To help out. Give food if it's needed. Elections are coming up at the end of the month. I can help with that. Make sure the school has what it needs."

Thank you, God.

She wanted to open her mouth and ask about the tax money, but there would be another opportunity.

"I'll show you around, if you like, Mr. Kirchner."

"If I can just stash my grip somewhere."

"Of course." Robert took up the bag in his hand.

"He cannot stay here." Clara's eyes went wild. "We cannot be in this house with a strange Yankee man. What would Mother Milford say about that? That her sons' wives would be at risk of defilement, and our reputations ruined in an awful way . . ."

"I'm just putting his bag inside, Clara. He can stay up at the teacher house with me." Robert stared at her as if she had two heads. She got a glimpse from Lucy and saw the twinkle dance in her eyes. Yes. She read it right. Clara wished the handsome soldier would stay the night there.

"I see." Clara, properly mollified, followed Robert inside the house. "I better make sure." Amanda tried to keep her lips from twitching. It must have been a long, long time since Clara was without a man. Still, this was a Christian school with Christian ways. If Thomas Kirchner were single, he just might be the answer to more than one prayer.

Please God. Help us and help her as well.

Lucy leaned over the portico and spoke to Amanda in a whisper. "I wonder if I might speak with you a minute."

"Sure, Miss Lucy. Am I doing something wrong with the baby's dresses?" Had she lost her seamstress touch? She hoped not. It was good work to do, and she would just have to practice more often to keep up her skills.

"No. I mean." She looked furtively over her shoulder. "I wanted to come by and tell you how sorry I was that you lost the baby. I prayed for your recovery. It must be hard to still be cheerful, surrounded by all of these children."

Tears started at the corners of her eyes, but she took in a deep breath to stop them. Still the tears flowed. She took out her father's handkerchief and dabbed at her eyes. Lucy patted her hand in understanding. "Thank you. I appreciate that."

"I don't feel the same as my sister-in-law, much of the time, but she's all the family I've got left. Except little

Franklin. And the girls. So I don't rock the boat much with her. She can be a handful."

Amanda sniffled and made sure to say absolutely nothing about Clara, while making sure to convey her gratitude. "I thank you for your concern."

"I wanted to say, though, if you need help with the little ones, I can do that. I can help you in the classroom. Little Frank could stay or someone else could take care of him, while I help you."

This was most unexpected. "Help me?"

"Yes, to gather the papers, drill the students. You understand. Help."

"That is very kind of you, Mrs. Milford."

"Lucy. Please. I want to do something valuable. And helping right this great wrong, that is God's work."

The surprise must have showed in Amanda's features. "A wrong?"

"I've never been comfortable with slavery. Never. We did not own any coming up. I knew what it was when I married Franklin Jr. And every time I've come, I didn't like it when you all . . . Well, I mean the Baxters waited on me. It was wrong. So I would like to do what I can to help."

"This is most unexpected."

"I have an education. I mean, not like you, Amanda, but I can read and write. So I can help."

"I have no doubt of that. It's just . . . is that what you want to do?"

Her blue eyes sparkled. "I would. Thank you."

"Well, then. You can help me teach as I sit. We can get school going after Election Day."

"Wonderful." Lucy laughed a bit and looking over her shoulder. "I better go get him."

She started to step away from their private conversation to retrieve her child, who was playing with some of the other Baxter children. Quickly, Lucy said, "I'm so looking forward to doing something and to being of use. As God would have us be. Thank you, Amanda."

Help came from all corners, she could see. She continued to hem baby Franklin's dresses, thinking that a little lemon juice in the cleansing water of these dresses would brighten the white. And she would try not to cry anymore.

Milford looked all tucked away when Virgil rode Pie in at dusk. Now to get him officially elected, they would hold an Election Day and pray the results would hold up.

But first, to his wife.

Pauline had told him she was up at the house when he rode there first.

He was not pleased at that, but neither was Pauline. "She's grown. I made sure myself she was healed up proper. She's been taking it slow, while you been gone."

Oh, that Pauline. She missed nothing at all. Virgil wanted to laugh, but he wanted to be with Mandy more.

"I'll see you tomorrow." He waved at both of the Baxters and went up the hill to his house.

Robert Lakey's lights were on in the teacher house and an unfamiliar blond man loomed in the window. What was going on in there? Mandy would know. He quickly rode by, on to his house.

He gave a shout out to disarm his wife. "Put the gun away, Mandy. It's me!"

He rode Pie into the barn and cared for her after her long journey. He came out of the barn, carrying his grip. The door swung open, and March came running out with all of the dogs to greet him. "You been behaving, March?"

"Of course, Papa. I'm eight. I know how to be now."

He kissed the top of her forehead. His daughter never failed to amaze him. The older she got though, the less she looked like Sally and more like him. How funny things worked out. "I see. Well, I'm glad to see you."

"I am too. You weren't gone as long this time, but this time, Mama was more sad that you were gone."

He stopped in his tracks. "Was it because she was sick? When the baby died?"

March nodded. "But she was sad because you were gone too. She missed you something awful. She cry, and she thinks I don't know, but I knew, of course."

He just shook his head, suppressing the desire to smile or laugh, which would only encourage March in her grown-up antics. "I see. Well, I'm back now. For a longer period of time."

"Praise the Lord," March shouted, and she danced off in a cloud of red dust.

When he faced the porch, Amanda stood there with her hair all out, down her back and around her head. This was the Amanda of his imaginings. All angular again and lean, but her coloring, the dimples in her cheeks, something was off. He strode up the stairs and took her into his arms, holding her to him with nearly all of the might he could muster.

Staying in his arms like that for a very long time, she didn't move, but slumped against him. He edged her back from him because he wanted to see her beautiful face and mouth.

The tears made streams down the side of her face and pooled in her dimples as they always did; wanting him to clench up his hands, because he had caused her this hurt. He had put this into her, and he would make it up somehow.

"Welcome home, Mr. Mayor," Mandy said with some cheer.

"Mrs. Smithson. What do you say we work on not parting for a while?"

The starch came back into her backbone, and she no longer leaned against him. She reached up and touched his face with her hands, smoothing his beard. "That would make me very, very happy."

"I would do anything to make you very, very happy, Amanda. I hope you know it."

She gave a little smile and made the dimples show. "You say that now."

"It's the truth."

"You haven't kissed me yet. That also makes me very, very happy."

He smoothed his hands down over her long hair and pulled her in tighter in his hold. "Me too."

He brought his lips down on hers, and she reached up to kiss him with surprising fierceness. Reveling in tasting her sweetness, he let his hand spread out on her back, kissing her back with the same kind of fierceness.

Mandy reached for more, like a hungry woman. He liked it that she fit to him and didn't have anything wrong or small to say. She was perfection for him.

When they parted, she smiled at him and reached back to contain her unbound hair in a fist. “You caught me in the middle of my braids.”

“You needing my help?”

“Always.”

“Wait for me, Mama and Papa!” March shouted out and ducked under their arms, running in ahead of them. Chuckling at her swiftness, they grasped hands and went inside to the home he had built.

Thank you, God.

In thanksgiving, he shut the front door behind them.

CHAPTER NINE

"If we had company, would that be a problem for you?"

This was the first she had heard of company since he had come home last week. What did he expect her to say? It would be a new experience—they had not had company at their home before, but she had to do what he needed. "Are you worried about me? I'm feeling stronger each day."

"And praise the Lord for that too, Mandy." Her husband looked up from working on his sermon. He still wrote in very slow, halting penmanship, but he insisted he loved the opportunity to practice his writing. "That was part of what worried me. They can bunk down in the guest room, and I'm thinking they'll not be much trouble. They're on their way to their home counties for the elections and wanted to stop through Milford to take a look at the town."

Amanda perked up. "Oh, they are fellow politicians?"

"Yes. One is in the House with me—that's Tunis. Henry is a Senator."

"Oh my. When will they be here?"

"Sometime this afternoon."

"Virgil, what are you saying?" She could not shoot up straight, as she wanted to since her loss of a more than two weeks ago. Instead, she pounded her fist on their dining room table in frustration. "We are having dinner guests—tonight?"

"Yes. And they going to stay over and attend church in the morning. They preach too."

Her hands began to sweat. "It would have been nice to spread the word about that, Virgil. I expect it will be quite a service."

Her husband shrugged his shoulders. "People should be coming to hear the word of God, not see a lot of show."

She stood slowly. "Of course not. Let me call March."

Vigil chuckled. "After breakfast? She so deep in the woods at this point, I don't know if she'll hear you."

She stepped carefully to the front porch and called her daughter. If it had been a typical Saturday, she would have had Saturday classes, but those were cancelled until further notice—until she got better. Still, now that she had Lucy helping at the school, maybe she and Robert would be able to have them again, so the adults could continue to learn how to read and write. Her falling ill wasn't their fault.

Fortunately, March came to her when she called this time. "Mama?"

"We're having company later today, your father says. I'm going to need your help getting the house and the guest room together, since I'm still not quite myself. I'm sorry you will lose one of your nature days, but it can't be helped."

"It's okay, Mama. I'm a big girl now. There's a lot I can do."

She held her daughter to her, and her fingertips tingled. March's quiet obedience made her feel better already. Ever since they had been alone together over the winter, March had taken on a little more responsibility for her than she should have, because of her condition. "March. Thank you. First, can you make sure we have enough scadies for pie?"

Her daughter smiled up at her. "That's an outside chore."

"Yes, start with that. Go down and get a bucket full. I'll make a pie for our visitors."

March ran off so fast the wind in her wake disturbed her skirts. She hoped there were some muscadines left. Folks would be wanting them to brew homemade wine—a constant struggle in the community. Pastor Virgil didn't want people to do it, because the wine caused trouble, but Mayor Virgil couldn't enact laws against it. The muscadine plants belonged on Milford grounds, so they were for everyone and he couldn't make a law about that.

Amanda took herself back inside and despaired of her housekeeping over the past few months. She had been in a fragile condition for so long, so her home had been neglected for a few months, more or less, but she could do surface things to have her house look good. She and

March would attend cleaning more deeply later in the summer.

By the time March had come back with the fruit, she had pulled together the living room, dining room, and kitchen. They set the pie to baking, put on fresh pole beans cooked with bacon rind, and set the fresh ham roast to roasting. They went upstairs to clean and freshen up the bedstead ticks with fresh straw and hay. They had only one bedstead, but two ticks. March stuffed the ticks full of fresh hay. It couldn't be helped. Maybe Virgil would be able to build another bedstead, if they were going to have politician company more often. The ironing board was set up in their hot kitchen and her braids gave her quite a turn, but she tied them back with a scarf and kept on pressing the white sheets with the flatiron, giving them the crispness they needed to be ready for company.

She heard Virgil give a yell, a welcoming yell, and took the iron off the heat. She managed to get many things ready for the company in short order of time and for the first time in a few weeks, instead of feeling sorrow at her empty arms and belly, her cheeks warmed at the sense of accomplishment she felt. She might not look very good, but she was presentable and things were mostly clean.

March came to her when she called, and thankfully, the child took the bed sheets up to the guest room to cover the ticks so stray hay and straw did not stick their guests in intimate places. Mandy pulled the red scarf off her head and stuffed it in her pocket. Smoothing down her dove gray day dress she had bought more than a year ago, she sniffed and a wave of satisfaction came over her, as it did when she took a test and knew she had done well.

Slowly, much more slowly than she would have liked, she made her way out onto the porch and waited patiently for her husband to introduce her to these two legislative giants.

The men stopped talking and laughing with her husband when she appeared. “Please. I know you are glad to see one another. You don’t have to stop on my account. Welcome to Milford, gentlemen.”

“Virgil. You did not say what an angel your wife was.” The stout gentleman came toward her and took her by the hand. “I’m sorry to impose on you just now, my dear. We’ll be away from you as soon as we can.”

“Oh, I wish you wouldn’t put it that way,” She tried to keep her voice light. “I’m healing. Honestly.”

“Beautiful.” The gentleman with glossy hair slicked back on his head, approached her. “Listen to her voice. Sounds like bells ringing. I don’t blame you for nabbing this one, Virgil.”

“Mandy, the big bear one grabbing at your hand and not letting it go is Reverend Henry McNeal Turner, who is running for the Senate. And the younger one trying to charm you, saying you sound like bells ringing is Tunis Campbell. Scamps the both of them.”

Once she let go of Rev. Turner’s hand, she made welcome for Tunis Campbell by shaking his hand, fine since they were in her husband’s presence and she had his permission. “Would you like some refreshments?”

“Don’t trouble yourself, Mandy. I’ll take these two and show them around town first, and then we’ll be back for dinner.”

“Virgil. You must give the guests a chance to reply.”

Tunis smacked her husband on the shoulder. "Lord, Virgil, you would have the manners of a bear if it wasn't for this wonderful woman. I'm feeling for these folk around here with you representing them, if you were fool enough to try to send her back to where she came from."

Virgil's eyes met hers, and unafraid, she met his gaze. "God knew how to set my feet on the right path."

"Well praise His Holy Name for that." Tunis intoned, laughing.

"Yes indeed." Amanda agreed.

The gentlemen were silent for a minute, but then Virgil coughed. Her husband was not one to show his emotions so publicly. She wasn't either, but she was glad that he understood more about the blessings God had provided them both with.

"Enjoy your tour of Milford, gentlemen."

"You get some rest, dear angel." Rev. Turner stepped his bulk off the porch and Tunis approached her to shake her hand again.

"Please. Don't overdo on our account." Tunis told her.

"Oh, come on." Virgil practically grabbed Tunis by the collar and everyone laughed.

Amanda waved them off and smoothed a hand down over her dress front where the baby used to be. It was good to see Virgil have some friends who were like him. Still, she hoped the gentlemen didn't tease too much. Her husband had a very tender side to him, and she didn't want that part of him to be revealed to anyone but herself.

That side of him belonged to her and her alone.

“Virgil, this is a lovely little place, but I’m telling you, bigger things await someone like you in Atlanta,” Turner told him as they rode their horses up the rise back to the house an hour later.

“And with a wife like that . . .”

“Tunis. Once more. Haven’t had the pleasure of meeting Mrs. Campbell yet, but I will make sure to talk on about all her charms when I do.”

His friend threw his head back and laughed. “Trust me; Mrs. Campbell would be liable to knock you upside your head if you talked about her charms.”

“Well, I hope to meet her someday.”

Henry shook his head. “You need to bring that wife of yours and come to Atlanta. You thinking it’s big time to be mayor here and have them ones in Crumpton coming to you for their services. It’s only a matter of time before they show how much they hate that.”

“Been happening since I been back here nearly four years,” Virgil reflected. Time certainly went by fast.

“You not listening to me. You got to make opportunities for yourself and that wife of yours. That’s in Atlanta, not here in this backwater town. And you say the family came back wanting that house?”

“The main house. Yes.”

Turner waved his hand. “That house ain’t nothing. You thinking it’s something because you country.”

“I followed the troops in the war same as you did, Henry. I know. I’ve seen things.”

“Well, then. Why stay there?”

Turner had a point. Mandy wanted it, and he wanted what she wanted. It was not in his heart to deny her. “It’s Mandy’s school.”

"It could grow more in Atlanta. There are more opportunities to get new students there. Let us talk to her and make her see."

They rode up to the barn, and it was Virgil's turn to throw his head back and laugh. "I want to pull up a chair and see this battle."

"Come on, then. I have much practice speaking to the gentler sex. She'll listen to me."

Virgil extended the hospitality of his barn to his guests' horses, and they lined up the care of their animals for the night. "There's the washing up stand over there. I'll start, cause when my Mandy gets to cooking, you'll be the one begging for mercy. Mrs. Turner made a fine meal and all, but Mandy got something special."

"That how she got you? She cooked?" Tunis patted the rump of his horse and joined his friend, who waited in the vestibule for Henry to tie his horse up.

"She did. Grape pie. I'll never forget it."

March came running to the barn entrance with fresh towels for them to wash up at the outside stand with. "Papa, there's more grape pie. I went and got them for myself."

Virgil patted her on the head and introduced his daughter to his colleagues and repeated to his guests, "Mandy made grape pie."

"Sounds intriguing."

"I think you are going to be the one who is persuaded, Turner." Virgil took up his towel and walked over to the stand where the outside stand awaited him.

"You mean to say to me you don't know how to talk to a woman? To woo her?"

"I'm one of those plain-speaking preachers, Turner. I don't have the charm as you do."

"You mean to tell me you made her do all the wooing work?" Tunis snapped a towel at him. "Are you a fool? Wait. The answer is yes."

The men laughed and made lots of noise, as the water and Mandy's good pine-scented soap made them smell much better than horses and male sweat.

They fell quiet when they went inside and sat themselves at his wife's table. She covered the table in a cheery red cloth and set up with the best dishes they had, china plates with a wheat sheaf in the middle.

When they stood around the table after his beautiful wife laid forth an excellent spread of sliced pork roast, fresh sliced peaches, tomatoes, okra and pole beans, Virgil wanted to make a triumphant shout unto the Lord, he was so proud of her.

Standing over the laden table, Amanda said, "I know better than to ask a table filled with ministers for the blessing. So, March will do the honors. Speak, child."

"Lord bless me and those of my race, make me humble to hide my face, make things safe for one and all, bless me Lord to be strong and tall. Amen."

Well, there was more than one female in his house who could take him by surprise. "A lovely prayer, daughter."

"Thank you, Papa." March curtsied and went out of the room until they were finished eating. It would not do to have a child at the table when there was grown-folks' company present. He knew his wife would be thoughtful and probably fed her before they came or would shortly after. Mandy thought of every single detail, part of what made her so special.

Please Lord, let her do what would be easiest on her.

He wanted her to recover, not because he wanted a son of her body, as everyone insisted he needed. But for her to be safe and to stay strong. Her strength and safety mattered to him—more than anything else. Losing her would mean the end of everything. The end of him.

Once they filled their plates and ate to their hearts' content of the food, Virgil knew his Mandy's cooking worked its magic.

For one thing, the men fell silent. Two other preachers? Had that ever happened in the history of the world? They ate and ate, and Virgil wanted to laugh as the food amounts reduced in serving size. When they became more filled with the goodness of the victuals, Turner said. "Ma'am. What a fine thing that you have the school in the house there."

"Thank you. But?"

Turner seemed disarmed. "Excuse me, ma'am?"

"You were about to say something about why I shouldn't have it in the house. I assume that's why you brought it up."

His Mandy's dimples deepened. Mandy stood up to Turner, not the least bit intimidated by him, and seemed to enjoy talking to him.

"Well, your husband indicated that you had trouble paying the taxes on the property."

"The house, sir, was a gift from Mrs. Milford to the citizens of Crumpton and Milford, held in trust to educate the children across the races."

"Ma'am. I have to say, I've been all over the south, all over Georgia. That won't happen anywhere."

"So what do you suggest, Reverend Turner?"

"Well, now. You can do several things. Move the school to Atlanta."

"If we moved it to Atlanta, the children of Crumpton and Milford will not be educated—the original intent of the school. That's the problem."

"You might sell the house and take the proceeds and build elsewhere."

"I'm sure my husband has told you of the family. They don't seem interested in selling. They only want to take over."

Turner folded his hands over his belly and seemed to nod off for a minute. Was he giving up that soon? Virgil's heart sank as he cleared the last of the pork from his plate, but then Turner's eyes flew open. "There are federal funds to provide for schools. You might petition for some of those. They might help you pay the taxes and begin to get the place in some shape—if you insist on having the school there."

"Where else?"

"The funds might be used to build another building and let those women have that house. I honestly don't feel the house is what you should be fighting for, ma'am. Personally. It's the school."

Now it was Mandy's turn to smooth her apron front down. "That is certainly true. Tell me more about these funds."

Turner rattled off more information about some magic school fund the United States Government had before the Civil War to set up schools. Virgil doubted that money still existed. The Civil War cost everyone so much everywhere, there was probably nothing left for schools.

"There is a representative of the Freedman's Bureau here. Would he know about these funds?"

"He might, but it's us you need, ma'am. It's the state that petitions the Federal Government for the money. Long as Georgia is in a cooperative mood to try to get back into the Union, we'll work for you. Together."

Mandy stood. "Wonderful!" She clapped her hands, and her gorgeous glowing skin and dimples were the deepest he had ever seen them. "I knew there was a reason for this political representation. Anyone care for grape pie?"

No one said anything as his wife turned around and went into the kitchen.

The three men looked at one another, and Turner whipped out a handkerchief to wipe his forehead. "I've not seen her like since we were negotiating the terms of the new constitution, Virgil. It's too bad she's not a man. She would out do any of us."

"I don't doubt it." Virgil sat back in his chair and folded his hands.

"She talk like that at you most days?" Tunis marveled.

"No. Just when necessary."

"And other days?" Tunis pressed him, leaning forward.

His wife stepped through the door holding the pie edged in golden brown and filled with bright purple filling, with her trademark brown crust grapevines overlaid on the pie.

Other days? That was his business. All by himself. He tucked his napkin into his neckband, because it wouldn't do to get any of the purple sticky goodness on his front. He did not care to make more work for his wonderful Mandy.

CHAPTER TEN

Virgil used his handkerchief on his neckband more than he normally did on a Sunday morning, thinking of Henry and Tunis attending him in the pulpit. He wasn't afraid of the smooth, polished city preachers coming and wowing the people, but his mind kept remembering, giving him ill ease.

His mind kept returning to what had happened at the last service, when Amanda had fallen ill. The memory of her slumping in his arms and going stiff might have been part of the problem. But here she was now, dressed in one of her dresses of darker blue, preparing for both the service and for the fish fry afterward, still getting around with caution, but getting around.

She dished up a hearty breakfast of grits, eggs and fresh biscuits with ham, that morning. "Do you want to call our guests in?" She set forth a dish of stewed fruit for the biscuits.

"Mandy, I just want to tell you. If I ain't told you. Thank you. For everything. And, I'm sorry."

She started her stiff-kneed walk to him, and he met her more than halfway. "Thank you, Virgil. You didn't have to say that. I'm happy to help."

He held her in his arms and felt her soft flesh yield to him, and he wished they were alone. But she was still ill, and he had to be so careful with her. He leaned down to kiss her and only got the most preliminary touch of her lips when the sound of hearty chuckling reached his ear.

"Now look, I don't never kiss Mrs. Turner until after my sermon. I find that it helps me to focus."

"Mrs. Campbell would have a fit if I wasted the Lord's precious preaching fire on a little loving before I deserved it."

"Hey, but Tunis, these two are still newlyweds. They don't realize the other one will still be around."

"Gentlemen." Mandy stepped in front of him, but still kept a hand on his arm. Still connected. Not ashamed to love him. "I apologize that we didn't have the second bedstead. Did you flip a coin?"

Tunis waved a hand. "I let Henry have it. He's as old as the hills."

"You old too, Tunis. Just in a different way. It was just wonderful, Mrs. Smithson."

"I'm glad. Please have a seat at the table." Mandy stepped away from him and the cold came in between them. What a healing balm it was to his soul to hold her in his arms.

"You all just lucky that I let you sit at my table, enjoying my wife's wonderful food."

Tunis rubbed his hands together. "God sure provided for you when he sent that woman south to put up with you. My, my, my."

"March isn't here to say the prayer just yet. So I will."

Virgil bowed his head and gave a heartfelt thank you to God for all that he had. His prayers needed an extra boost today. *And please, dear Father God. Help me. Help me to reach the heart of your flock today—just before the election. Help the people to know how important they are, so change can come to us all.*

He lifted his head and Tunis's hand shot out for the big bowl of grits and red eye gravy. A load lifted from his heart. God had heard him—he felt sure of it.

Virgil had gripped her waist a little too tightly this morning. He had nerves. His hold on her hadn't hurt her or anything, but he held her just that much closer, almost as if she were a good luck charm. Despite Pauline's objections, she wanted to be that for him. So she sat up front, right where she always did. Besides, it was not a good idea to bring up memories of the one time when she had sat in the back and gotten ill. She would never sit back there again.

Given the way Virgil went on about the travail faced by Noah in the time of the flood, comparing them and their cause as those who were chosen to be on the boat as opposed to the rest surrounded in sin, she was right.

Part of his nerves might have been the showy aspect of his friends, who read special scripture, but Virgil's fevered prayer made it plain—this was his house and they were visitors. Special visitors, but still, visitors.

"Let's sing special for our gueMy Hope is Built on Nothing Less.'"

Despite her recent illness, Amanda rocketed to her feet. Virgil knew that was one of her favorite hymns, and she was ready for it. They had gotten through the first verse when there were shadows in the door, and she turned to face them. Robert Lakey came through the door with Tom Kirchner and the Milford daughters. Lucy smiled and nodded at her, gave her a little wave, but Clara stepped in on Kirchner's arm no less, nose turned up as if something were smelly.

Virgil cued the congregation to keep singing, and she loved him all the more for it. Mrs. Milford used to come in the middle of his services all of the time, after she finished attending church in Crumpton, and she guessed much the same was happening here, even though none of them, with the exception of Robert, had visited before. What were they there for?

When they finished singing, the congregation fell completely silent. Some of them had not seen the Freedman's Bureau agent before, and doubtless, they wanted to know who he was and what he was doing there.

Mr. Kirchner was dressed in a brown suit, and unfortunately, did not know enough not to step his big feet into the aisle while the spirit of God dwelled in His house. Her husband's beautiful full lips tightened a tad more, and she wished she could kiss the tension from them.

"Reverend Smithson. May I have a word with your congregation?"

"We're in the midst of celebrating a worship with the Lord, sir." Virgil chewed off each word with precision. Tunis and Henry, sitting in special chairs behind Virgil, approved. Henry Turner seemed like such a jovial fellow, but this latest development caused a frown to appear between his eyebrows.

"I apologize for disrupting, and beg your pardon. Please, believe me. Mrs. Kirchner raised her baby boy better than this."

Amanda's lips thinned. What did this man want? She opened her mouth to encourage him to make his peace known, but Pauline had something to say, as she usually did.

"We got to praise the Lord," Pauline shouted out. "What you got to say? Unless it's some testimony about Jesus, we going to praise him now!"

People giggled, someone started to hum, and others picked up the tune Pauline had referred to, clapping their hands.

"A testimony? Sure. I'll give a testimony."

The congregation fell silent again. This was unexpected. How did a white man offer up a testimony? What would he know about it, that he should come in their midst and offer up testimony, let alone know what it was.

Jack turned to the congregation and spoke. "I've only been here a few days. I have to say, Milford is one of the most impressive places I've seen. The town is neat and orderly. You have a lively church service here. Everyone seems to be engaged in valuable enterprise."

"It's our mayor!" Someone shrieked in the back.

"We don't mean to disturb anyone; we got God's peace here." Pauline asserted.

"I see that, ma'am. I'm from the Freedman's Bureau, and I . . ."

"I heard tell that your help brings trouble to folks. What about that? We don't want trouble times here. We got what we needs."

Several Baxters agreed with Pauline, clapping their hands in appreciation. "I see that. I just wanted to make sure things go smoothly with your election process on Tuesday. To make sure the school stays strong."

People fell quiet then. Amanda knew that was what everyone wanted. *Please Dear God, let the school stay strong.*

"I don't mean to cause any trouble, but if I over-watch the elections on Tuesday, I can make sure those things happen. I just wanted to present myself to the community, so you know who I am. We want to make sure all will go well."

Please, dear God, let the election go well.

People in Crumpton were voting too. All that was needed was for some trouble to be stirred up between the two. Her stomach clenched at the thought of trouble. Jack continued, "Folks over in Crumpton might not be happy at your elections, since they aren't allowed to vote."

"All they have to do is say they'll support the Union." Henry Turner interjected. "No one is trying to stop them from voting."

"Well, yes. I know. But will they do it? And allow things here to go smoothly? That's the question. I'm willing to stand by here and help. If you'll have me."

Tunis and Henry gave side-glances to her husband, and she knew what he was thinking. She tried to will the answer to him. *Say yes. Say yes.*

Virgil stood. "It's an interesting time you pick to come and speak in the Lord's house, Brother Kirchner.

But if you are willing to come and work on behalf of the Lord's purpose, we're willing to have you. Thank you for your service."

Her husband nodded at the man, sure Jack Kirchner would turn his brown-booted feet toward the door and take himself back down to the Milford house.

But he didn't.

He stepped forward and offered his hand to her husband.

Virgil's eyebrows raised up at the gesture, but Henry Turner hovered at his elbow, making gestures to him that he should shake the man's hand.

And he did. Then Henry and Tunis.

Something even more remarkable happened then.

Jack Kirchner walked back up the aisle and sat down. Next to Clara who wore a strange smug expression on her pretty features that Amanda did not like. However, Lucy smiled and nodded at her.

A feeling of hope surged in her heart. Would they, could they, dare hope that everything would be all right? She did stand then and began another chorus of "My Hope is Built on Nothing Less", the song they had just sung, to bring forth the surge of hope that she had in her heart. Virgil smiled at her and joined her in the song, as did the rest of the congregation. She had no doubt.

Tuesday would be a landmark day.

The house was still and quiet in the middle of the night. Her husband had reached for her, and insisted on holding her in his arms.

"I'm not rushing you into anything, wife. I want you to be in the best possible shape for yourself. It was selfish of me to go after you before. I won't do that to you ever again. I'm stronger than that."

She perched herself up to look down on him, ready for him to complain that her skinny elbows stuck him in his chest. He didn't, maybe because her elbows were not skinny any more. They might never be any more, since she'd had a child in her belly. "So strong that you don't want me anymore?"

"So strong, Mandy, I'm going to always choose what's best for you. And it's better that I hold you."

She laid her head back down on his broad chest, so happy he was taking this time to linger with her before they went back to sleep.

Then, the clear clarion sound of the town bell rang into the night.

They both sat straight up in bed and looked at one another. Without a word, they dressed quickly.

No need for talk, or for wasteful words. They needed to know what was happening in the village, because whatever it was, the mayor was needed.

Amanda looked in on March, who sat straight up in bed. "Stay asleep. We'll be back soon."

"I want you to stay here with March."

"Are you sure you don't need me?"

"I may need you to make some food. Please Mandy."

Still, she took a shawl and wrapped it about herself in the night to look down over the bluff. Something was on fire in the town. "Take care of yourself, husband." She reached up and kissed him on his precious lips. "Hurry home to me."

"I will."

It didn't look like a building was on fire. The flames were central in the town square. Still without proper care, the fire could quickly spread to other buildings—the church, the smithy, maybe even Milford house without care. The flames had to be put out.

Amanda put together a breakfast for her husband when he came home. It was close to dawn and he would be hungry when he returned.

Her thoughts came to fruition when she watched Virgil drink deeply of the hot coffee and wolf down the ham and grits before he could talk.

"It was the flowers in the town square. They're all gone. Not going to look very nice for the Election Day frolic."

"Terrible. How do they think it happened?"

"I wish I could say. Maybe a loose coal from the smithy."

She shook her head. "You were shut down. It was Sunday. Isaac didn't open the shop. How could it be?"

"Someone set it on purpose, then." His jaw firmed.

A chill ran through her. "Who would do something like that?"

"Don't know. I just know we got to get the square looking just so tomorrow in advance of Tuesday."

"I agree. I'll go out and help when the sun comes up."

Virgil paused in his eating. "Don't want you to work too hard."

"I won't, husband."

He shook his head. "I don't like the looks of it. Not this close to the election. Too many changes might be going on up in here to suit the Crumpton folk. You never know what might be making them do things."

"They can be unpredictable."

"Wife. Henry suggested something. I want you to hear me. Understand?"

Amanda sat down with a cold cup of coffee in her hands. "Of course. What did you discuss?"

"He's still thinking you should move Milford School to Atlanta."

She took a sip of the strong coffee and arranged her features in a way that did not convey her disappointment. "I thought he was saying something to you about politics. What could he care about my school?"

"He thinks it's dangerous here and you trying to do too much."

"The nerve of him coming up in here and seeing what I do in one day and deciding. Husband, the school is for Milford and Crumpton. Mrs. Milford gave us the house, gave us the land to make a school."

"Taxes, expenses are eating all of that up. We don't have no choice. Let those daughters have it. Henry told you about the money the government might have. And there's plenty up in Atlanta who need to learn—I've seen them. March could have better opportunities at a job up there, and you can start a school there."

"Virgil. The Baxters live here. You want to leave the Baxters here, without an opportunity to learn?"

Her husband stood. "You been teaching for the better part of two years now. They got some learning. Now the Freedman's Bureau is here, they might start another school, get other teachers. Not you."

"I'm tied to them. They're my family."

"You're my family, Mandy. You and March are the only ones I got in this world and I can't put you in no more danger. No. After the election, I'm taking you on to see Atlanta, so you can see for yourself what Henry is talking about. All I'm asking is for you to think about it."

She stood up, a storm raging inside of her. "I can't believe you are asking me to give up everything I know and have worked for over the past two years. For something I don't even know."

"The capitol is going to be in Atlanta, Mandy. I've got to get there if I'm going to be doing all the politics you wanting—to get money for schools and to help Milford. It's the only way."

"I don't think it's the only way. I just think you want to get away from here. I don't. It's the only home I know. I'm not leaving just on Henry Turner's say so, I don't care who he is."

She broke away from his hold and went upstairs, her cold, bare feet slapping on the wooden stairs in their house. She needed to get dressed to see what needed to be done in the town square as soon as the sun came up.

Couldn't Virgil see how she wanted to be home? She and her father had moved so often when she was a little girl. Couldn't she have one opportunity to stay in the place where she felt comfortable? Where it was home? How could he ask her to go somewhere else and make an opportunity out of something strange, someplace strange?

What would the Baxters say? What would they think if they left them behind? She grabbed a fistful of her pillow in her hand and punched it. She could not leave Milford land. She would not abandon the school. There had to be some other way to get the taxes paid. After she fixed the town square, she would figure out what to do.

Then it occurred to her.

She could have to go back to Oberlin and meet the devil, but if that was what was required . . . she would do it.

Please, God. Not that.

Closing her eyes, she laid down on the bed, and the weakness spread thorough her limbs. The town square needed her, but first a nap. Her mind danced active, even as her body needed rest. She was tied to this place. She could not leave it behind if there were other choices to be made.

What else could she do?

CHAPTER ELEVEN

A few hours later, Amanda left her husband as he slept. He needed his rest too, and she was not about to bother him. She donned an old patchwork quilt dress Pauline had helped her make, she liked it best because it had some of the leftover pieces of her wedding dress in it, but it made for a fine dress to wear when she had chores or had to be the outside.

Besides, she had to be in the town square when the sun came up.

March tiptoed out in the hallway. “Mother, where are you going in the darkness? It might be dangerous.”

“It’s almost time for the sun to come up, little one. If you want to come with me, best get dressed quick. Your papa is resting.”

March didn’t say another word, but went away to slip into her third-best dress. It wasn’t the dress Mandy wanted her daughter to wear for digging in dirt garden-duty, but if March helped to do the laundry, she would learn the more difficult way to be more selective of the clothes she wore for the task she was about to do.

Her father always taught her in that way, by experience, not by just telling her things. Even after more than two years, tears stung her eyes.

What would he think of me catching me here wearing an old dress about to go dig in the dirt?

He certainly hadn't raised her to be a slave, but technically, she had been born one. And ever since she found out that truth about herself, she determined to never, ever, forget. So, even as she recovered from the loss of her son, it was more important to remember who she was and to remember the lost ones.

The sun touched a corner of the sky pink as she and March walked out of their door, past the teacher house, down the hill to the town square.

The horrible sight greeted them. Every single rose bush and crepe myrtle tree was singed to a nose-clearing black crisp. It was as if whoever did this intended to burn the life from the heart of the town. Not another building, business, or the church was touched.

"No." March whimpered.

Part of Amanda wanted to cover March's young eyes and protect her from this hideous sight.

Something turned over in her belly and she steeled herself. She had to know this persecution. March grew up in this place, of this time and place and would, no doubt have to learn to replant and restart numerous times in her life. No better time than starting now.

"We'll start over here in the corner and see how far we get before people come to help us. We'll start with the little plants first."

"Why would someone want to do this, Mama?"

"Someone who doesn't like the idea of what we are trying to do here."

"What are we trying to do? Maybe we should stop it."

Amanda pulled herself down closer to the ground to face March. "There's a new day coming. Different from the day where you might have been someone's little workhorse, not able to go and play with the dogs or gather scadies in the woods as you like to do. You would have had to learn to obey and nothing else. Because of people like your father, Mr. Tunis, and Mr. Henry, times are changing. Those days are over. Even just us in the small act of replanting the town square, we're going to show whomever did this those days are never, ever coming back. We'll be back here for the picnic in just a few days to celebrate that. Do you see?"

March's eyes still carried fright in them and seeing her eyes go red with that emotion moved her. The trowel in her hand slipped a bit, but she grabbed a hoe. "Let's get to work, child. You'll see. It will be pretty again."

The red clay did not yield up the burned plants that easily. The hard character of the land surprised her. Still, the rigidity of this land might have been the very kind of motivation she needed after someone had done such a petty thing. She wouldn't give up easily either. Digging and examining the plants, she knew that if they were trimmed down to just the basic plant and the roots, they would grow and flower again. The flowers stood for their resiliency.

The pink dawn spread across the sky and warmed into a Georgia spring morning. Other townspeople, on their way to the fields, brought small hand tools out with them and without a word, got on their knees next to her to help. Some of her pupils came, as well as many Baxters to help her in her task. Soon, the scorched plants formed a pile in the corner of the square and one of her uncles, Basil Baxter, came forward with his wagon and mule. Virgil came down in time to load up the wagon with the old scorched plants. When the mule pulled slowly away with its heavy load, Virgil put an arm around her shoulders and squeezed her to him.

Amanda closed her eyes, feeling the pain form into tears underneath her eyelids, but she would not cry at this. No. Whoever did this would have to try harder than this to break them. She knew, in a way most Milford residents did not, what it meant to be a free citizen. She would not cry. Their right to live as they pleased must be protected.

Tuesday, Election Day, dawned bright and clear. Amanda, feeling much better, made a pie and a cake to go with the chicken she had fried. With fresh peaches, a pan of cornbread and some of the pickles she had put up last winter to occupy her time while Virgil was gone, she knew they would have a feast. Despite the sadness that had dogged her heels lately, she put on a new dress, a pink one sprigged all over with little flowers. There may not be flowers in the town square as of yet, but she would bring them to the square.

Of course, she made a matching dress for March, but her pink was slightly more pastel, less bright than Amanda's. Virgil pulled the wagon around for them, jumped off the box and helped March into the back, along with all of the goodies she had made.

He came and stood over her, very handsome in his brushed dark-brown broadcloth suit. She smoothed down his lapel and he stopped and captured her in his arms. “You look more like yourself today, Mandy.”

“Meaning?” She raised up an eyebrow.

“Means this.” He reached down and touched his lips to hers. She leaned into him and met his lips, yielding to the waves of pleasure soaring through her. Now she understood how someone like her grandmother would be able to have twenty children. She had not been successful in birthing their son, but even that pain and cost to her body seemed to have disappeared in the wake of his kiss, his scent of licorice, and his smooth, sure touch on her waist. She wanted to take off her bonnet right there and let him run his hands over her braids, right then and there.

A faint sound of a harmonica playing sounded in the distance, and March murmured behind them. “We don’t have all the day, Mama and Papa. Let’s go!”

Her husband lifted his head from her slightly and sighed. “You hear your daughter, Mandy?”

She smiled at him. “I heard her. I think she wants cake is all. Wait until she gets older and she finds someone like you and knows what this is all about. She’ll be sorry she interrupted us then.”

Virgil frowned. “She’ll be much, much older.”

Amanda laughed, in a way she had not in a very long time, and moved toward the box with her husband helping her up into the front seat. They had to set an example by showing up to the picnic on time, and she didn’t want to ruin anything for her husband’s chances, even if he were running unopposed. They needed every single vote of support in the town, to show the people in the Georgia

State Legislature, especially the Democrats, they were on board with liberty.

Virgil reached over to squeeze her hand as he pulled off, driving with the reins in one hand. Oh yes. He felt the same way. Despite the growing heat of the day, his warmth reached the tips of her toes. *Thank you God, for bringing me here to love this man.*

She meant every word of it.

In spite of his daughter's worry that they would be late, they weren't and were among the first families there in the beheaded-looking town square to arrive. Virgil watched as his wife directed some of her younger cousins in making rosettes and bunting from fabric scraps. What a wonder she was. Everything she did helped to make things better and lent a patriotic air to the proceedings.

Isaac emerged from the shop and brought forward the wooden voting box made of pine and polished to a heightened shine. He set it on a corner of a hastily erected picnic table and stood back proudly to watch his nieces decorate the square. "What a fine morning."

Virgil clapped a hand to the shoulder of his partner and declared, "I appreciate all you done. Where's Pauline?"

"She wanted March to help her carry her goodies and things. Now March is here. I expect she'll be here directly."

"Good. Women can't vote, but I'm sure she wants to be here for the picnic."

Isaac shook his head. "No. They can't. Too bad for it. Only other person as good at running things around here is Pauline."

“Don’t go telling her that.” Virgil shook his head. “We would never hear the end of it. God knows his business.”

They smiled at each other, and Virgil knew that Isaac knew they would be busting a gut if they were younger boys. Clear enough who ran things around here. Some things didn’t need to be said.

“Are there any more tables?” Mandy swirled to him in her pretty pink dress, a frown etched on her smooth features.

“We’ll bring ours down from the house.” Isaac beckoned to a few of his Baxter nephews.

“That should be enough, thank you, Uncle.”

“It’s fine. You look mighty pretty today, Amanda.” Isaac gave him a meaningful look. “I hope you knows that.”

His wife smiled. “Thank you.”

“Don’t we need that table down here?” Virgil shouted. “You all can’t carry it, let me know. I’ll bring it down here myself.”

Isaac laughed and two Baxter nephews followed him back to his cabin. Isaac was always telling him about showing his wife affection and love, and whatnot. He did what God lead him to do. Couldn’t do any more than that. It was too high a price to pay in putting too much of yourself into one person. Learned that lesson the hard way when he was young. Now he was an older man, he had seen many things and was going to start a new way. He couldn’t see his way clear to pouring all of himself into another woman, even if it was Mandy.

His heart gladdened to see her pink skirts moving around better than before, organizing the baskets and keeping them all in order on the table her uncle brought forward. It was important to do that—not everyone's cooking was the same. And praise God, best of all, she wasn't stiff or sad or dragging in her movements, she was back to herself.

Of course, it hurt him in his heart that his wife couldn't have her heart's desire. Mostly, he lived on seeing her happy. Complaining would do no good. God had given him a delightful family. What more could a man want? Isaac mostly worked at the smithy, and there were plenty of Baxter nephews to bring in. Younger than him, she would learn. Sometimes, making changes was not worth the cost of the sacrifice. She'd come around to his way. She taught the children in the schools—she saw babies all the time.

He riffled through his pockets and reviewed his notes as more people began to arrive and leave him mostly alone. Nothing like the power of a few precious sheets of paper. He understood. The paper and the fact that he had made crooked scratches on the paper surprised him too. He wouldn't have had that without Mandy.

Looking up from his perch on a wooden bench, Mandy had stopped all of her swirling about and had gotten one of those Baxter babies. Thank the Lord for that, because maybe holding one of them would make her stop wanting what God had denied them.

Then he stood up, getting himself ready to move to speak to the crowd and his view of his wife changed. She didn't look satisfied to hold that baby. She looked hungry. Her eyes looked like ghosts lived in them, like Pauline's eyes had whenever she had trouble with a baby.

If only he didn't have this speech to give, he would go over there and give that baby back to its mama. He knew. He would take her to Atlanta with him when he reported the results of the Election Day. She would see the workings of government, and she would be fine. Like a honeymoon. They had never taken one. It had been work, work, and work, from the first day of their marriage.

His hands gripped at the papers harder, to get a firmer hold of his words. He would do better by her.

"Good day, friends. Got some things that need to be said, before we get moving on with this box that Isaac carved for voting purposes."

Out of the corner of his eye, Lakey, Kirchner and the two Milford women moved in. What were they doing here? Was Lakey here to vote? Made sense when he thought of it, but he hadn't counted him as a voter. Guess he did. Probably could have been nicer to him.

Virgil cleared his throat and the crowd quieted. "Some of you met my friends Tunis Campbell and Henry Turner when they were here. They're men of God as well, and they say that times are changing for the better. Someone, as we could see by what they did here in the town square, don't like this change. It's too bad for them. We get our say into this box for the first time in our lives and I want us to pray. Pray together for a new and better understanding. Pray for guidance."

Everyone, even the troublesome Milford women lowered their heads at his command, and he opened his mouth to speak, but the hard, slamming thuds on the ground from a bunch of horses rose up through his feet and he lifted his head to look around.

Horses. Coming fast.

He moved to the sound at the edge of the town square and squinted to peer up the bluff to see six horses making their way toward the gathering.

The crowd, no longer in a prayerful mode, watched on with him as those horses thundered down the hill toward the town. Virgil reached for the pistol at his side, always kept there these days. Still, he approached the riders—looked like some of the Crumpton boys—in peace.

"Good day, you all come for some of our fine eats on the town square today?"

Tom Dailey moved his horse forward to the front of the pack. He didn't ride as fast as the young ones did, apparently. "If you inviting us, Virgil. Always glad to oblige you."

"Thought you would be over in Crumpton voting, rather than coming over here."

Dailey's cold blue eyes rested on him. "What now, you think we didn't do right and vote for you? That what you saying?"

He matched his gaze. "Nope. I'm saying I thought you had better things to do than to be worrying about what's going on in Milford."

Kirchner had come to stand next to him but stayed silent. Virgil didn't need the help of some made-up government official who had a job his father give him, but Dailey did look extra mean today. Probably extra drunk on scadie wine. "'Course I'm worried about Milford. It's where you from."

"We was about to pray. You welcome to get off of your horses and pray with us. Plenty of food to share if you want to watch the proceedings."

"There better not be no proceedings. Your people here, 'cepting for you 'cause you had your freedom papers, and these white ones over in here, best be the only ones in that box."

"Well, why don't you join in and see us vote." He did his best not to grind his teeth together. A featherlight touch landed on his arm and Amanda was there next to him. "Plenty of food for all, Mr. Dailey and cold teawater. Lemonade." She spoke out in a firm strong voice.

"Pretty northern wife you got. Got plenty of spunk about her, Virgil. Plenty. Okay. We do what you say. After all, you our state representative. Got to watch the proceedings."

He gestured toward the smithy. "Your horses can stay in the smithy. Wash up stand is in there too. We'll wait until you come on out."

Every eye in the Milford town square followed the men as they went into Virgil's place of business and took their horses in behind them. Mandy's hand gripped his sleeve.

"Why are they here?"

"I don't know. Best to keep an eye on them here rather than them causing mischief elsewhere."

"I don't like it." Kirchner spoke up.

"If they here for what they say, it will be all right." Virgil put his other hand on Amanda's and patted it. "It'll be fine."

"Your hand is cold." Mandy grabbed his hand and held it firm.

He squeezed back. “You warming me is all I need, Mandy.”

They both watched as the men came forward from the smithy, with slicked down hair plastered to their heads, their faces and facial hair only half the way clean.

Virgil lifted his hand. “Bow your heads and give your thanks to God.”

His heart rang in his ears, and he prayed as he had never prayed before for God’s love and protection to bless this day.

They sorely needed it.

CHAPTER TWELVE

"Hard to believe all this celebration is for just two people to vote." Tom Dailey spoke out and some spit got onto someone's pickled green beans.

Dear Lord, please help me to respond kindly.

Amanda busied herself scooping food onto a tin plate. Chicken, pickled peaches, the spit upon green beans, bread, a slice of grape pie and a piece of plain cake. She tried to keep her head lowered so she didn't meet the ice blue eyes of Tom Dailey. She really tried. Maybe she should give thanks the harsh cold of the winter had kept Tom Dailey in his store in Crumpton. Whenever those cold eyes roamed over her person, she wanted to cry. Maybe she missed her baby, that little piece of Virgil, who had been her protection while he was gone, and without that, she felt too vulnerable under this man's close scrutiny. Even though Virgil stood not far from them—watching her.

How was she to hand him the plate? An idea came to her. She lifted her head and held the plate out. "We love to celebrate in Milford and want to send off the new representative in style."

He snatched the plate from her hand and some green beans landed on the ground, sending up a nose-clearing scent of vinegar. "That's all it better be, northern gal."

Fortunately, he deemed her unworthy of any further conversation. Dailey moved off to a bench and she served the next Crumpton guest. Pauline stood close by her and March between them. Better they be the ones to serve the company, and not expose any of their young Baxter nieces to the gaze of these men.

When the last one had been served, she took a deep breath. Virgil headed to the front of the crowd and raised up his hands.

"Thank you all for attending. And for making this supreme gesture of God's gift of liberty to us. This is Milford. Our town."

"You better believe it is!" Pauline shouted out into the crowd, and they all laughed, Amanda noted with relief. All of them, except five.

She stepped over to Tom Dailey with a small bag. "Fixed you some cake for your journey bag to Crumpton, Mr. Dailey."

He spat in the dirt at her feet. "Who says we going anywhere?"

"Unless you plan to move here, I suppose you'll be leaving at some point."

He stood up. "Virgil. Come up here and get your Yankee woman."

Virgil wrapped an arm around her before she knew it. "She only offered you some refreshment. I don't see the harm in that."

"We want to see the voting."

"Did you cast your own ballots?" Virgil asked gently, but with intention, pushed her behind him, and she stayed there in his protective shadow. He knew what would be required for them to vote. An oath of allegiance to the Union.

"Of course we did." One of the Crumpton boys shouted out. "We want to see yours."

Amanda knew him for a liar, but her husband gestured. "Well, let's get down to it."

Calla Baxter brought forth a long ledger book and opened it to a brand-new page. Virgil signed the ledger. Then he picked up the pen that Calla brought forth and used it to sign the accompanying paper ballot with only one name on it. He blew gently on the ink to dry it and with great solemnity, dropped it into the slit at the top of the wooden box.

"My residency makes me eligible as well." Lakey came forward and signed in as well, voting in the same deliberate way her husband had.

Calla Baxter closed the long book and took it back to where it had come from inside the smithy. Isaac followed her with the wooden box.

When she had disappeared, Virgil turned to the Crumpton boys. "You have seen liberty at work here. If you will leave us to our merriment, gentlemen."

"Tom, you said all them others would be voting before us." One of the boys complained.

Amanda wanted to laugh at the frustration in Dailey's eyes. "Tessie been watching the store too long. She get liquored up, I don't know what my sales be. Let's get on back."

He stepped forward and snatched the bag of cake out of her hands, almost knocking her over if she hadn't been standing right next to her husband, who held her arm. "You're welcome!"

Her voice rang clear throughout the spring afternoon and Tom Dailey did nothing but grin as he gripped at the cake. "I heard tell of a young one coming, Virgil. Must have had a mighty amount of fun with that."

"I hear tell that the woods are full of danger at this time of day, gentlemen. You best get going." Virgil rested his hand on his pistol and she knew he made sure Tom Dailey saw where his hand was.

"Well, indeed. We would be expecting a visit from our representative before you get on back to Atlanta. And his smart Yankee missus is always welcome." He made an exaggerated movement in bowing to her, and her lunch roiled in her stomach, wanting to come back up again.

"Good day. Let Mrs. Dailey know we are concerned for her health." Mandy nodded and spoke quietly.

Thankfully, some of the smaller Baxter boys brought the horses out for their unwelcome guests, so they could leave that much sooner. Amanda's eyes met the kindly blue ones of Lucy Milford and knew she had cued the boys to retrieve the horses. "Wonderful voting day." Tom Dailey said as he seated in his horse. "Be seeing you."

Virgil said nothing but his attention focused on the leave-taking of the men and waited until the sound of their horses' hooves had retreated completely from Milford. "While we vote, I want a man on each corner of the town square with his gun to keep the area protected. When it's your turn, you can come back, and someone will cover you to vote."

Calla and Isaac moved with more purpose and intent in retrieving the items the first time around and Calla opened the book to the freshly inscribed page with two names on it. Virgil intoned. "When you have your say in the government, know that you are a man. These are the actions of men, and that you are men. We don't need outsiders telling us about our manhood."

Tom Kirchner sat down beside Calla and helped her keep the tally, signatures and votes straight as fifty-four other males in the Milford town square voted, signed as best as they could, swiftly and without incident. *Praise God.*

Now she could stand back and watch the dancing.

His heart sank a bit when someone brought out some musical instruments and they began to push back the tables for dancing. Amanda's pink skirts still swirled amongst everyone else's and made her stand out, like a pretty rose of some kind, but he didn't want to pick her, if she didn't want to be picked.

Had they ever danced together? Ever? He didn't remember, ashamed to admit he had never held his wife in his arms and moved together to music. He moved forward to take her hand in his and stop her organizing, but Lakey got to her first. Because Calla had started dancing, Jack Kirchner was left with the voting ledger and box alone.

Freedman's Bureau or not, he didn't know Kirchner, so he went to see to the security of the items with him. Fortunately, it was a square dance and Lakey didn't have to touch Mandy or anything, but instead, she whirled about the town square, making it look alive and vibrant again. All because she was there.

He turned to see how the Milford sisters took all of it in, but Lucy sat with her son, holding him to her and helping him clap his baby hands along with the music while Clara frowned.

He showed Jack Kirchner where the ledger and box were stored away in the smithy until the counting could occur. Kirchner spokc to him and pointed. "I'm going to get out there and whirl Mrs. Milford around a bit."

"She's looking mighty unhappy at this moment."

"I told her to come here. It's part of my job to be here. She wanted to just sit on the porch and watch from there, but I knew it would be better to be closer. She'll be all right. She just needs to dance a bit."

She needs more than that. Virgil did not speak his thoughts aloud and did not say any more. Jack Kirchner had a point. Some places thought dancing was sinful and not of God. He never held to any of that. When they emerged from the smithy and Kirchner stepped forward to her, the sour look on Clara's face had disappeared and a new look of shy acceptance replaced it. Such a change for old devil woman, but she actually looked like a human woman while Kirchner whirled her about on the town square. Nice.

His wife had moved on to another partner, one of her tall young male Baxter cousins, teaching him to dance as much as he was having a good time whirling her about.

Hadn't done much dancing in his life. How did you ask your wife to dance when you hadn't danced before? What did that look like? Fresh shame washed over him at the kind of husband he had not been to her. He was not like other men though, so it was hard to be that way when he wasn't.

Walking over to where the musicians were playing, he stopped for a moment to listen, and Pauline made a beeline for him.

God, please, I'm trying to be better.

"Wife looking like she having fun being treated like a woman, 'stead of an old workhorse."

"You look like you was having a good time too, until you decided to get into other folk's affairs and come over here to me. Where's your husband?"

"Oh don't you worry none, Mr. State Representative. My man is never far from me. He takes care of me, for certain."

He surely did. That was one thing Virgil admired a great deal in his protégé. He was not shy about how much he loved his Pauline. She hadn't had the easiest life, so it was a great day when Isaac had become brave enough to confront his long-held feelings for his older sister's childhood friend. When the bad times came to an end, and the former enslaved people were allowed to marry for real, Isaac and Pauline were the very first couple he had wed. An example to all.

Unfortunately, they had no children. He at least had March. More proof that they were fine.

"You taking care of your wife, while you away?" Pauline swayed in exact time to the music as the group of musicians changed to something slower.

"Might take her with me. Seems as if Milford might need someone new to lead."

"What you say?"

"What you think I'm saying. Thinking about appointing Isaac as my deputy mayor. He can be here doing things, instead of Mandy. She's my wife. She belongs with me when I'm up in Atlanta."

"Well. High time you got some sense in you, man. I'm glad to hear it."

He couldn't help but smile. Pauline was one of the few people in the world who could stir him that way. "Glad to meet with your approval." His eyes followed Amanda as she went and sat down on one of the wooden benches, fanning herself. Her eyes glimmered and she laughed at something her nephew said, her eyes brightened by the fun of dancing.

"You do fine. But you going to do even better for our people. Amanda, she's got all of that education, she can help you better up there. We going to miss you, but we'll be fine back here."

Pauline turning serious on him surprised him, but she was right. He said, "Only thing, she doesn't want to go because of the school."

"Well, now. You got to help her see that she's getting help at the school. Mr. Lakey's there. Miss Lucy helping out."

"I told her she could even teach school there."

"She could. No need in that going away."

"I just need her to do as I say."

Pauline smacked him on the shoulder. Now the serious was all gone. "You been married to her for most two years, and you still ain't learned yet? She's never going to do just what you say without reason, fool. Gentle her into it. She love you, although I don't know why. Maybe she ain't as smart as she make out to be."

"A wife is supposed to obey her husband."

"Now you a bigger fool than I thought you were. Maybe we 'lected the wrong person in the state house. Long as you showing her how it's going to help the both of you, she'll go. Do it right, 'stead of all this—'I'm the mayor and the law of this here town and I say let's get on to 'lanta.' Do it better than that."

"You might be right."

Pauline smacked him again. Her smacks didn't hurt, exactly, but she sure had strength in her arm. "Of course I am, man. Look, she come down here and discover we are her family. I still think she's trying to get used to it, but she feel obligated to bring all of us up to where she is. It's a nice thing she doing, but she got to see that will take some time. She got folk here helping. It won't hurt her to take a few years to go on up to Atlanta with you."

The move--temporary. A good way to put it. He nodded his head. "You got wisdom yourself, old Pauline."

"Of course I do. I know you both better than you know yourselves is why. Start off by being nice to her. Go on and dance with your wife."

"Ain't no one dancing out there now." The alarm in him made his fingertips tingle.

"We join you in a minute, I'm just resting myself afore I get my Isaac out there. Go on, Mr. Representative." She elbowed him and once again, the strength she possessed had never failed to amaze him.

Hands in his pockets, he crossed the town green and moved to his wife, standing over her. "Excuse me, J.D. I need to have a word."

Young J.D. Baxter and everyone around them cleared a pathway for him. Yeah, people tended to do that when he was around. Mandy stood up and her eyes still shining, looked at him. "Yes, husband?"

He reached a hand out to her, keeping the other one firmly in his pocket. "Would you care to dance, Mrs. Smithson?"

The pleasure on her face dawned like a bright morning sun. She put her small hand in his and squeezed. "I would be delighted to."

The musicians had not changed their tune, but kept up a slow rhythmic meter as he escorted Mandy out onto the town green. Time to face up to the music. He took his other hand out of his pocket and wrapped it around her waist, pulling her to him.

She caught her breath, and he gave her a grin as he interlaced fingers with her. Then, they moved to the music in a slow rhythmic way, as old as time itself. "Something wrong, Mrs. Smithson?"

Her heart fluttered on through the pink. He knew because her flutters matched exactly the ones in his stomach. Same beat. "Why, Virgil. You . . . You can dance."

Some of his townspeople clapped as Isaac and Pauline joined them on the town green again along with other couples. "Thank you, Mandy."

"Why didn't you tell me you could dance?"

He edged back, looking into her dark eyes, and the dimples appeared on her face again. "Would it have mattered to you?"

"I don't know. Maybe." Now she dimpled in confusion, and he liked it. "Why do you ask?"

Now it was his turn. "I don't know. Truth to tell, I haven't done much dancing in my life."

"No? Well, you certainly wouldn't know it. You're doing very well."

"I learn things fast." He pulled her in to him again, holding her close, relishing in sensing her discomfort at his capabilities.

"Some things." She murmured into his broadcloth coat and he spread his fingers out on the small of her back.

"When I get you home, Mrs. Smithson, you shall pay for your sassiness."

"Oh, really?" Mandy answered and her eyes flashed as she looked up at him. "I'll pay the price. Whatever you deem necessary, Mr. Smithson."

Only the necessities of courtesy and the expectations of his newly held position, prevented him from taking her home now. He said nothing, but danced on with her. Why had he taken so long to know this kind of pleasure in her arms? He would never put it off again. Not anymore.

Was he feeling the strange feelings of pleasure again or… did the earth move with horse's hooves again?

His gaze turned to the bluff. Dear God, the Crumpton boys thundered onto the town square once more. He broke away from his wife's warm hold, and Tom Dailey's cold blue eyes regarded him again, this time from up high on his horse. The music had stopped and all of the couples dancing slow in the dusk stopped to see what was going on.

He kept his voice casual. Easy. You gentlemen need help? Again? A shoe for your horse perhaps?"

"Come to get the Milford results, Virgil. If it isn't too much trouble."

"The election will be certified tomorrow." Jack Kirchner stepped forward from where he had been dancing with Clara. "I'll make sure of it, gentlemen. It's part of the work of the Freedman's Bureau."

Dailey spat in the dust. Liquored up again, do God. "Part of the work of the Freedman's Bureau is to ensure that the freedman has everything and we got nothing. That's what you doing here helping out with that school."

Mandy's small hand disentangled from Virgil's, and she broke away from his hold. He wanted to reach for her again and keep her by his side, but she had moved forward of him too fast. "We want all of the children of both towns educated. That's what Mrs. Milford wanted. To prevent these kind of confrontations. Now there's no more cake, but pie instead. Will you have some?"

Dailey had pulled out his gun, and Virgil went quickly to his. *God please don't make me use this gun.* He would if he had to, but he didn't want to. Out of the corner of his eye, Isaac stepped forward with his pistol. Virgil pulled Mandy back toward him. "I said state your business, Dailey. It takes up mighty precious time to keep coming here from Crumpton, and I know you have your place of business to run."

"Just wanted to make sure everything is being handled properly."

"It is, Mr. Dailey. Just bringing our nice day to a conclusion."

"I'll be by in the morning with the results, I assure you Mr. Dailey." Jack Kirchner said.

Why had he said anything? It was better to not to remind Dailey that Kirchner was there. When would northern people see sometimes silence was best?

"You better be. Fine. Tomorrow then." Dailey edged his horse back onto the road and shot his gun into the air.

Virgil wanted to sag in relief, but he couldn't. Next time they had an election, they would keep it quiet. So many people wanted to celebrate the inclusion into liberty, but celebrating liberty was too dangerous close to the bad times.

Mandy's scream, the same scream that echoed in his ears from when she lost the baby sounded out and his heart froze in his chest thinking about the shot Dailey fired into the air by way of threat. He pulled his wife to him, but nothing was wrong with her. *Thank you God.*

"Noooo," his wife screamed at the stricken, slumped body of Pauline and the spreading circle of impossibly red blood on the front of her dress.

CHAPTER THIRTEEN

Virgil had never needed to call upon God to give him this much strength as God could give him.

He was having to hold up everyone else. Got him to feeling like Atlas in the storybooks Mandy read to March.

Mandy, on one side of him, cried all day and night. She kept murmuring, "She was the first one who was kind to me when I came here." Her words prodded Virgil into remembering how he had treated his wife when she first came to Milford—not a fond memory.

On the other side of him was Isaac. Quite and stoic, something about the way his friend held himself in the face of the loss of his beloved wife was not right. He couldn't put his finger on it, but Isaac's silence chilled him.

March, in front of him, went around taking care of everyone, something that a child didn't need to be worried about doing, but it was almost as if she had taken up Pauline's place in some strange way.

All of that, and he had to have some words of comfort to say for her funeral tomorrow.

Yes, God. Strength, more and plenty of it.

Three days after the election, when he went down to the cabin, and Mandy stood there cleaning dishes, her brown complexion grayed out, he had enough.

He took her by the elbow, gently. "We going home."

"I have to wipe these plates for folks to eat . . ."

"Now, wife. Home."

The few people who were in the cabin, sitting with Pauline in the middle of the large room, as she lay smiling in the coffin that Isaac had so hastily built just after her death, looked up at them.

They smiled, but said nothing.

Mandy put the towel down and wiped her hands down her front. "Good night, everyone."

Calla came up and took up the towel. "It be fine, child. We finish up here. I expect you all have a lot to do before the service."

"We do." Virgil guided Mandy to the door. "We see you later. March. Over here now."

March skipped over to him instantly, and he took his family to the wagon and made sure they were secure in it, before he hitched Pie to the reins and took off for their bluff.

"Why did you do that?"

"Do what?" He shouted as if there was a lot of noise to talk over. Actually, there wasn't. Ever since Pauline slipped from them three days ago, Milford had an eerie sense of quiet about it. No. Things wouldn't be the same without old Pauline telling them what to do.

"Take me out of there like that."

"I'm your husband. That's why."

"I know that. But I needed to help."

"You . . . Mandy, you just got over being sick. You want to get sick again?"

"No, but if they needed me . . ."

"I'm not going to have it so you get sick again. That clear?"

"Yes."

Her one word and folded hands struck him because she backed down too fast. A feeling of incompleteness ached in his middle when he pulled up to the front of the house.

"I believe we have some cornbread and buttermilk left if anyone wants to eat." March's little voice came to them, kind and deep.

"I'm not hungry," Mandy said without any tone in her voice and tried to jump off the wagon box before he could help her. He came around to her side just in time and caught her as she jumped off, helping her up the steps to the house.

"If you aren't hungry, get on upstairs to the bedroom and lie down on the bed. I be up there soon as I put the horses away."

He let her go in. Turning, his gaze rested on March, who had worry etched between her pitched up eyebrows. "Daddy, she hasn't eaten since this morning. That's why I said what I did about the cornbread."

"Fix a bowl then and leave it on the table. I'll get it when I come back inside after I put Pie away."

March followed him as he guided the horse to the barn. "Will she be okay?"

"She will, honey. It's just going to take some time, is all."

A little cry erupted from his daughter. “I been losing all my mamas, and I’m only eight years old. I don’t want to lose the only mama I got left.”

He reached an arm out to his child and pulled her to him. “Mandy’s going to be fine. You’ll see. She’ll be all right. You go on and make that bowl of cornbread mush. I’ll help her eat some.”

March wiped at the salty white tracks on her small features. “Okay. If you say so.”

“I do. And you know I’m right lot of the time.”

“Well. Mostly.” March agreed, and his lips twitched. Oh, how inappropriate to laugh in the midst of all of these great tragedies they had endured lately. His daughter warmed his heart though, for sure. “Papa?”

“Yes, March,” Virgil worked quickly to put the wagon away and to get Pie down. Why didn’t she go in to make the mush?

“I been thinking. I want to sing when we have the services. We would always sing together, and I want to sing for my Pauline one more time. You think I can?”

Sing? His child? Besides church? “Well it’s going to be in the church, so if you sing a church song, it would be okay.”

“You mean a song like they sing in the fields?”

His hand slipped off of the curry brush he used to take care of Pie a bit but he righted himself. He didn’t have the greatest of fondness for those songs, because they reminded him of the bad old times and the ways they would reassure themselves, but that was Pauline’s music. She sang it in the fields and she would see to it that they sung some of it in church. “They our work music. Shows the Lord we work for him now." Pauline's words had always knocked down every protest he ever had.

She had that way of making the best sense in the world and her loss knifed him in the gut. He rubbed his midsection, willing the pain away. He had to be strong for everyone else.

"Is that what you want to sing, child?"

"Yes." March's eyelashes fluttered about on her cheeks.

"Well, then, that's what you sing. One song. Make it good."

"I will. Thanks!" March rushed off to the house, twirling around as she did to that invisible music that played in her head.

A song would make tomorrow's combined church service and funeral very interesting then. Still, he had never heard her sing, and she was only a small child.

What harm would it do for a child to offer up a song? If she didn't sound well or made people uncomfortable, he would go to get her and set her down next to Mandy. It would all be fine. But first, he had to make it fine with Mandy first.

When he reached the bedroom, Mandy was so still on the bed, he thought she was sleeping. He brought forward the bowl full of cornbread mush and worked himself around to her side of the bed and she kept still, tears sliding into the pillow.

"Mandy, come here, wife."

He helped her to sit up.

"This place makes no sense to me. Why isn't anyone sad about this? Why isn't Isaac mourning his wife? Sometimes, I feel like a stranger and I don't belong here, but never more than this, when I'm grieving for my friend and no one else is mourning her."

He sat himself down next to her on the bed. "You see what old Pauline looked like up in that coffin?"

"I helped Calla wash her."

"I know. Calla was glad you helped her. Old Pauline, she just smiling, and everyone was talking about it when they look at her, didn't they?"

"Yes. They thought we did it somehow, but that's how she looked when it happened. We didn't, I mean, you can't fix her mouth like you want once she was gone. She was smiling. Is that supposed to help me to feel better?"

He rubbed her shoulders and felt her relax under his touch. "Maybe some. I suspect she was getting to heaven to see all the ones what went before her. She saw Jesus. She didn't have to stoop over to pick cotton no more, no more worries about Mrs. Milford. She seeing Sally again."

He didn't trip over his words when he spoke about his first wife. Pauline and Sally had been best friends. Mandy choked, "She was just getting to the point where she could read from the Bible. I wanted her to have that."

"I know she was glad you taught her so much. You need to be real proud of that. She was determined to get all the schooling she could, but she still had to keep up with everything in her land and her house. It was joy for her. But she really wanted the young people to learn, didn't she?"

"Oh yes. She say she would pick double and harder, so they didn't have to. That's what she wanted."

"So you keep doing as she wanted you to do, Mandy. She smiling on that. That's why she smile."

"And your election. That's what she was saying. About how you got elected and you would be big time in Atlanta. She was proud of you too."

He put the bowl down on the nightstand and pulled his wife's feet up onto his lap, unhooking her shoes from her feet. "These things matter to Pauline so. The faster we get away from the bad old times, the better she liked it. And now," slipping off one of her shoes, he fixed his gaze on her. "Now, she as far away from them times as she can get. No use in crying when someone leaves, Mandy. We learned in the bad times, anyone can leave at any time, in any way. There was never no use in crying tears. It's just the way that it is."

"March cried when I left."

"She a child, Mandy. She never came up in the bad old times in a real way."

"Well, she's not crying now. I'm worried about her."

He let the other shoe drop on the floor. "She worried about you too. She told me to bring this up for you. Say you hadn't eaten since this morning. That true?"

Mandy nodded her head and the fear for her health struck him again in his midsection.

"That's not right, wife. You got to keep your strength up. Please." He leaned over her feet and passed her the bowl.

She took the bowl into her hands and began to eat the mush in small spoonfuls and swallows. "Don't you have to do a sermon for her?"

"I'll think of something. Don't worry. I can't have you getting sick on me. When this is all over, I want you to come to Atlanta with me."

"The school session was going to start up again. And the courthouse date for the tax bill is next week."

"We'll stay for the courthouse, but we going to have to figure the school out. Somehow. I want you with me, wife."

She lowered the spoon into the near empty bowl. Lifting the bowl up to him, he took it from her, placing it back on the nightstand and began to rub on the soles of her feet. Mandy closed her eyes in ecstasy and leaned back on the pillows of the bed again. "All that doesn't stop me from wishing she were still here. How can we make these things work? I didn't know how hard all of this would be."

"I didn't either. I guess we are learning."

"Just like we'll have to learn how to do without her."

His heart ached for his friend Isaac, in remembering those long cold days ahead of him, without the sunshine of his wife to warm him. The thought of the missing warmth contrasted with the cold knot of anger and hatred he had for Tom Dailey. It was his careless gunplay that killed Pauline, and the judge in Crumpton dismissed it yesterday as an accident.

He had to go to the capital for sure by next week, but he needed to make it clear to Isaac he could not go after Tom Dailey. God would see to justice for him.

He was sure though that he, and only he, understood how nearly impossible it would be for Isaac not to seek revenge. Whatever he could do, he resolved to help his friend deal with it. As God would have them do.

The gray heavy sky opened up and rained buckets of cold water down on them for Pauline's homegoing service on Sunday morning. There was nothing of the hot picnic weather that had allowed them to dance and frolic upon the burned town green just days before. By the time they arrived at church in the wagon, they were all drenched. No amount of oilcloth covering them seemed to help keep them dry.

But they weren't the only ones there. The church was filled to the rim with souls from Milford, Crumpton, Daviston, and all up and down Liberty County. Everyone knew Pauline and they all knew she was a martyr for a cause. Even Robert, Clara, Jack, and Lucy came and stood along the back wall. Clara's bored expression rankled her and Amanda set her jaw straight to endure the woman's presence, but she was there. The recently closed coffin rested at the front of the church. Virgil had some of the Baxter men, not Isaac, nail it shut. He would not have the service over Pauline's open coffin and she could understand why. Still it was the weirdest thing. There was no crying, no shouts or moans. Just eerie silence.

What is wrong with you all? Why aren't you crying for her? She wanted to take up her weeping task again, but her past few days of mourning, as well as crying for her baby before that, left her utterly devoid of tears. She had no moisture left in her soul, but she wanted someone, anyone to take up the task for her.

It certainly wasn't going to be Isaac. He stalked around looking as if someone had slapped him in the head. Virgil went to the front of the church, and Amanda and March took their rightful places in the very first pew at the front next to Isaac.

Virgil went to adjust himself, and all they could hear was the water sluicing down the sides of the church building. But the water wasn't getting in—she knew. Her husband had built this house of God too sturdily for that.

She felt a surge of pride for him, replacing some of the ill feeling she had at his too-strong strength. He hadn't even cried when she lost the baby, and now he seemed just fine when he had to eulogize his friend, this woman who had taken on the job of raising March when her mother was sold away from Milford. Pauline deserved better.

She put her arm around March and smoothed down the braids she had just rebraided, facing the coffin with the smiling Pauline inside.

"Sometimes, God asks us to pay a heavy, heavy price for what we have. Dear God, would we have ever thought a week ago that we would be here now, under these conditions to mourn the loss of our great friend, Pauline Baxter? We sometimes bring our cares to God and ask him, are there some sacrifices that are too much? Are there costs that are too much to bear? Can we endure these great pains and sorrows of life? Job did. He endured them. He endured all of the losses and pains and still was a man of God."

Amanda tuned her husband out. Job? Was that the best he could do? The whole thing about how other people had it worse? No, that is not what she needed just then. No one had it worse than she did. In a few short weeks, she lost her baby and her friend. Who knew if she would ever have either of those relationships in her life again? Would she lose the school as well? No. There were some costs that were too high to pay.

She was not satisfied right now. God had to show her something. He needed to prove to her she would be all right without Pauline. But she didn't see how.

The pain intensified behind her eyes, but she kept her silence. Her husband preached on, and she didn't want him to feel humiliated at her moans anymore. Nor Pauline, who smiled on in her coffin, even as they would put the wooden cover over her, take her out into the slave part of the Milford graveyard, and put her in the hole they had prepared for her. She closed her eyes to see if that would ease the pain.

Suddenly, she felt a lightening in her hands and March slipped from her grasp.

She opened her eyes to see March, standing before them in her black dress that was getting too small for her, she noted. March folded her hands in front of her, the picture of obedience.

What was she doing?

Amanda started to move forward to pull the child back to her, away from Pauline's coffin when March opened her mouth and began to sing.

A grown woman's voice came forth from her daughter's mouth—the sound of a woman fully immersed in experience, love, sorrow and life. The sound went up her spine like an otherworldly shock. God was here and he knew her pain. He would heal it.

In that moment, the rain stopped, as March sang on in her shockingly adult voice, "Soon I will be done with the troubles of the world, the troubles of the world, the troubles of the world, Soon I will be done with the troubles of the world, I'm going home to live with my Lord!"

And just when she thought she had no more left, the tears came.

CHAPTER FOURTEEN

God had given them the gift of March. The entire church was stunned to hear the child singing about Pauline getting into heaven to be with her God, and not having sadness anymore from the bad old days, or not being able to have babies of her own. Amanda's sight cleared up from her blurry tears as some of the Baxters behind her began to whisper.

"That's Pauline's heart talking."

"Her heart talking."

"Child, yes. She was responsible for March when she was just a young baby. She the one Pauline couldn't have for herself."

"Indeed. Her heart. How she get to sound like a grownup woman? She only eight."

"You questioning the ways of God?"

"No, indeed. I never heard anything like it."

Neither had Amanda, and up in the pulpit, Virgil's handsome features were arranged into a perplexed look. Who was this March, singing her heart out, when all the child wanted to do was dance free in the woods?

March leaned her head back as the song built to a crescendo, and the last note of the song practically leapt from her and grabbed at the throat of everyone in the church.

No one said anything.

March returned to sit next to her, grabbing her around the waist. “I knew they wouldn’t like it,” she whispered.

She recognized the need to be strong for her daughter. No more weeping and a-wailing. “Honey, that was the most beautiful thing I’ve ever heard.”

“It was?”

The emotions clogged her throat. She couldn’t say nothing, but then, in a clash of noise and sound that made her almost jump in her skin, the applause, the clapping, the shouting, the screeching of approval came from every soul crammed into the church. March grabbed her around the waist and began to cry, and Amanda rubbed her on her back.

The release March needed. *Thank you, God.* She knew March had the emotion in her. Pauline had been the only mother she had known for years. Poor March. She had gotten handed around so much. She would never abandon her.

Her husband, up in the pulpit, wore his storm look on his face and for the first time she knew, he seemed unsure of what to do. Amanda nodded to him to show him she had March in hand.

He gestured to the bearers, and they came to carry Pauline’s coffin out. Everyone stood up to see the coffin of the kindly woman carried up the aisle of the church and out the front door. To applause.

Was the applause for Pauline? Or March? It was hard to tell.

March's song had ended the service. Could anything more be said?

Isaac went first behind the coffin. She and March lined up behind him, and as they walked out, hands reached to March in approval and petted her as if she were some special charm to help them recover from Pauline's death. March kept clinging to her skirts and crying, so Amanda had to mince along behind the coffin for the both of them.

Oh God. How will we make it without Pauline?

Still they had to. They had the responsibility of caring for Pauline's heart. So they would find a way.

"Where on earth she learn to sing like that?" Virgil asked her as they readied for bed after that long exhausting funeral day.

"Husband, I'm sure I don't know."

"I never heard anything like that before."

"Well, it's clear that March has a gift."

"I always knew her to be a little peculiar, but this . . ."

"Peculiar? Did you talk to her about it?"

"No. I didn't. Not sure what to say."

Amanda slid into the bed next to her husband and snatched some of the sheets away. "What a thing to say. Tell her it was beautiful, and that you enjoyed her singing."

"Seems like trouble to say what's already there."

"Well, you have to tell her something. You can't act as if it didn't happen."

"I'm still thinking about what has to be said."

"She'll be grown, seemingly, by the time you get done thinking about what has to be said."

"She say Pauline taught her?"

"Yes. That's what she said."

"Old Pauline. Always the last one to get the upper hand and leave you thinking. Even from beyond the grave."

Amanda leaned into him. "Yes. That was her."

"Last thing she tell me was to take you away from here."

She sat up in the bed, jabbing him with her elbows. "What? Why would she say such a thing?"

"Say we need to go off somewhere together. We never took a honeymoon."

"That's true." She clutched the sheets to her, covering herself. "But this is just about the worst time for something like that. The court's going to decide about the taxes next week and I have to be there."

"We don't have the money to pay them taxes. Those girls came back to get what their mother gave them. Let them have it."

"Let them have it? Just like that? Give up the school?"

"Mandy, I didn't say nothing about giving up the school. Just move it. Move it to Atlanta. That's where we going to have to be anyway."

After everything that had happened over the past month, this was just one more thing, one more mountain, one more burden to bear. She drew in a shaky breath and lay back down on the bed, careful not to touch any of her husband's body. "Mrs. Milford. She gave that house and the land to educate the people here. Not in Atlanta. It's not about me. It's about them. If I leave and move the school, then it becomes something else that she didn't intend."

"Mandy. We need to get some rest and stop this fussing. Anyhow, don't you see that if those girls win in court, you are free of all that foolishness?" He turned over on his side away from her. "Women. Can't see nothing."

"Yes, I'm a woman. And what of it? You, great state representative, don't seem to see the importance of educating these people here, maybe because they aren't your family."

"They are the closest I'll ever get to one, because they are your family. And March's. Isaac too. Why do you think I'm going up to politic for them? You act like I don't care."

"Well, you don't. From what you are saying about moving the school."

She turned from him too. That should fix him.

He slid off the bed in his long johns and grabbed up a pillow and blanket. "You needing me, I'll be out in the barn."

"Fine then," she choked out. This was not what she needed. But sometimes, it seemed to her Virgil didn't always understand what she needed. She had resolved to do better about telling him, but he looked busy a good part of the time, so she wouldn't bother.

She climbed back out of the bed and got down on her knees next to her bed and bowed her head. She didn't know what else to do but talk to God. *Am I being a good wife? How can this all work for us? Do I have to give up the school? What am I here for anyway? How do I help March? Show me the way out of this, Lord. Let me do your Will. In your name, Amen.*

She slid back into the bed and the cool of the sheets burned her. Virgil was right to leave the bed—there would be no rest there for anyone that night. She picked up her pillow and went down the stairs. She looked over at the red davenport where she used to sleep in the days before they were married. It was comfortable then, but would it be comfortable now?

You belong with your husband.

She knew it was the right thing, but something inside of her still burned. *Well, I can go out there, but I don't have to stay with him.*

The warmth of the April evening sank warmth into the balls of her feet as she navigated the stony, well-worn red path between the house and the barn. It had rained that day, but every drop of water had already cleared up. So typical of Georgia. The mud already was on its way to becoming dust.

By the time she reached the barn though, the edge of her white nightgown was all red and her feet were dusty.

There her husband lay on a quilt on the haypile. He was wide-awake. "Thought you was a horse thief come to steal Pie. You lucky I didn't shoot you." Virgil gave half a smile, and the air of tension and anger between them eased.

She wasn't one to waste time, so she addressed it right away.

"Are you angry with me, Virgil?"

He reached out to her and she went to sit next to him on the quilt. "Why are you saying that?"

"You're the one who came out here, Mr. Smithson. Not me."

He put his arm around her and drew her in close to him. She could feel his heart beating inside of his chest. Her proximity that made him excited too. She loved that she had that impact on her very own husband. "Things changing so fast, sometimes I feel like my head about to swirl on off."

"I know. So much loss."

"I'm not asking you to leave for no long time, Mandy. It would be a couple of years."

A couple of years could make a difference of a lifetime to children who needed lessons, adults who needed to learn how to read. "If March has this gift, then Atlanta could be a place where she might cultivate it."

A look of surprise dawned on his face. "Wasn't thinking of that."

"I am. She's our daughter. You have to think of these things."

He squeezed her to him. "And I married you to think of these things."

"That's not why you married me."

"Well, maybe not, but it worked out that way for me." He reached down and captured her mouth with his own. She could hardly breathe for the tingles of pleasure that raced around in her arms and hands at the way they were loving each other on the barn haypile.

"Why didn't we ever come out here before?"

"I don't know. People having fun in barns all over Milford."

"Do they have this much fun?" Amanda stood up and drew her nightgown over her head so that he might see her as God fashioned her.

He groaned. "Are you fixing to drive me out of my mind?"

"Whatever works, Mr. Smithson."

She knelt back down on the quilt, he quickly covered her with his own body and Amanda stretched out, enjoying the sensation of his fully clothed body up against her. He covered her lest she be cold, she knew. Even though there was still a lot to talk about and uncover, she was more than happy to open herself to him, happy to be loved by such a man.

Days later, he resolved to do one more thing before he went on to drive Mandy to the courthouse in Crumpton: Check on Isaac.

His bereaved friend had taken to spending nights in the smithy. "I don't want to be in the cabin without her."

Virgil understood this. Some. Sally had been sold away from Milford for a long time before he had found her, so there was no real place that had been "theirs" for very long. Still, if something terrible like what happened to Pauline happened to Mandy, he would be driven out of the house by the aching, echoing loneliness that happened when you lost somebody. Still, he had a plan in mind for his friend. If he could stay awake.

Lord, that scamp wife of his wore him out, keeping him in the barn these nights.

Isaac was hard at work when he came in—as hard at work as he had ever been in his life.

He did not seem to notice him standing there. He kept pounding away on some poor item. Virgil approached him slowly, not wanting to startle him. With hot tools in his hands, Isaac required a gentle approach.

Isaac's red eyes met his when he came in. He startled a bit. He didn't expect his friend to look so lost, so vulnerable.

"What you want?"

His hoarse voice surprised him too. "I just came to talk to you. See how you doing."

"You worried if I was working or not?"

"I didn't say that, Isaac." Something inside him lurched. *Help me Lord.* This wasn't going the way he expected at all. Isaac kept up the happy side, and he was the one who greeted all, stayed pleasant to all, most especially him—his boss. Still, he recalled how Sally's death hit him. He knew. He understood.

"I'm here. Plenty of horses need to be shod."

"I wouldn't blame you none if you wanted time off."

"And where you going to be? Going off to Atlanta or something? We don't keep this business going, Crumpton folk liable to go elsewhere. So I work."

"You right. I'm glad you are here. Taking care of the smithy. And Milford."

"Doing that too. It's all fine. I don't need no talking."

How could he approach him now by saying he wanted a favor? Good Lord, the man acted as if he had already dumped the weight of the world on him.

"Isaac, I wanted to take Mandy with me to Atlanta this time. Count of we never had no honeymoon before."

Isaac's gaze unnerved him as he pounded out something—Virgil couldn't make it out—it wasn't a horseshoe. He plunged the iron into the bath water. Looked like a leaf of some kind. Isaac was making some art.

There were blacksmiths who did that kind of thing, but it wasn't his way. Interesting how Isaac had his own take on the whole business. Never occurred to him to make something like that.

"Not a bad idea. Pauline say you need to do that after Amanda got sick and all."

"Yeah, well, I wanted to leave March. With you."

His words got Isaac to stop pounding so hard on the next bit of metal.

His friend put down the tools and took in a deep breath. "What do I look like? A mammy? I can't take care of no little girl while you up in the capitol with your wife."

"She be in school most of the day. You worried about meals, Calla probably cook."

"I got more food than I know what to do with. I expect I'll have to be throwing some out when it go bad. I don't have no time for a little girl."

"You don't want to stay in your cabin, you can stay at the house with March instead. In the guest room."

"I don't want to. No. Thank you. Let her stay with Calla and them."

"She want to stay with you. She say so."

Isaac shook his head. "She liable to start singing again. I can't have that."

Virgil threw up his hands. "I'll tell her not to sing. Okay?"

"Pauline sing like that and she taught her everything she knew. I don't want to hear it."

"I understand."

Isaac stepped back from the heat of the forge and went into the office all of a sudden.

He knew what he went back for. His idea didn't work. Turning on his heel, he prepared to leave the smithy and ride on over to Calla's to see if she would take care of his daughter. He bent to pry a stone out of Pie's foot. Lord, he hoped people wouldn't treat March as if she were a haint from the spirit world. People got to be outcasts real quick if others didn't understand what they were doing. No kind of life for his child. Maybe Atlanta would be the better place for them, but he just wanted to get away with Mandy for a week or so . . .

He swung himself up on Pie's back and Isaac emerged from a shadow of the smithy. "When you all leaving?"

"After this courthouse thing is over on Tuesday. Wednesday probably."

"I was going to that anyhow. I come on home with you all and bring my things to stay. If that's okay. You can get an early start that way, if you want."

"Sounds fine to me. I'm appreciating it."

"March, she . . . She was what Pauline and I couldn't have. You know? It's not fair to leave her too alone at a time like this."

"That's what I was thinking. And I wouldn't be going to Atlanta unless I had to."

"I know. I understand. And Pauline, she believe in you."

"I know she did."

"I'll see you later then."

"Isaac?"

"What?"

"What you making?"

"Flowers. For her grave. I ain't no good at gardening. I can do some ironwork, so that's what I put over there for her."

"She would like it fine, Isaac."

"I guess. I get back now."

"Fine. See you soon."

He had some mayoring business to attend to, but it could wait until tomorrow. Something very powerful in the marrow of his bones made him want to go up that hill to the house and see what his wife was up to. She wore him out, but it was so much better being alive. Guiding Pie up the hill, he smiled to himself, knowing if Pauline were here, she would smack his shoulder to show her approval.

CHAPTER FIFTEEN

Pulling the wagon up to the courthouse in Crumpton, Virgil questioned his judgment once more in coming to the courthouse. Why was he here? Why had he brought her here? This would all end up hurting her. The family would be hurt. More and more, he could see the truth of what Henry and Tunis had told him. They had to get out of Milford.

Another fancy carriage pulled up, and Charles, the big-time flunky for the Milford family and jack-of-all-trades, came out and opened the door for the four adults inside: Clara, looking saucy and triumphant; Lucy, who seemed sober; Robert, with his usual cheery emptyheaded way and Tom, all about business. The men waved at him, but he ignored them to grab Mandy's hand to hold it to stop her from waving. She frowned at him. "Why did you do that?"

"This is the courthouse. Not a tea party."

He bustled his wife, Isaac and March up to the gallery to watch the proceedings down below.

"Why do we have to sit up here? Why aren't we closer to help support the gentleman who on our side?"

Virgil spoke through tight lips. "I don't know that he's on our side as much as he's on Mrs. Milford's side to keep things the way she wanted them."

"Mrs. Milford would be appalled at all of this." March's words echoed throughout the nearly empty courtroom. "She wanted me to have a place to go to school. Why are we here?"

He had to hold himself back from reaching over Mandy to cover his daughter's mouth, so instead he said with iron in his voice. "Keep that child quiet."

Lucy turned around and looked up at them in the gallery. She gave a little wave to March and Mandy, and he could barely hold back from scowling at her. He was not about to start trusting that woman. Better to have someone like old demon woman, who firmly believed they were nowhere near as good as she was. At least someone as vain as Clara was honest.

Mandy leaned to their daughter and gave a half-hearted reprimand.

He reached over to grab her hand in his. "Listen. However this turns out, you come and be by my side in the capital. At least for now."

Mandy drew her hand back. "Why Virgil?"

"We took some wedding vows, and you said you would obey me as your husband."

A frown crossed her pretty features. "I don't remember saying that."

"Well, maybe you should have. You just don't know how these things work out. I want you to promise me."

"And March will come with us?"

"Eventually. We leave her here with her uncle for now, find some place to live and then we'll come back for her."

Tears welled up in Mandy's eyes. "I'll do as you say. I just don't like ignoring the words of a dying person. Besides, I'm a lawyer's daughter. I know the law."

He squeezed her hand. "Mandy. Mrs. Milford did this to be spiteful. She knew what the outcome would be. She wasn't no fool. She did this to her family to be mean. To us to be mean. Now I'm telling you . . ."

A loud call disrupted him. Her dimples puckered in confusion. He hated to be this blatant about it, but she had to find this out.

"The court is in session!" A red-face round gentleman dressed in a suit, screeched his call out to the room.

Their inevitable fate took several long hours to decide. Yes, this was all part of Mrs. Milford's spiteful way to make her daughters-in-law earn their property, by sitting in the courthouse on their behinds on hard wooden chairs for a long period of time. Still didn't change the outcome.

The Milfords got their house back, and they had to leave.

Amanda sat there in stunned silence, and Isaac put a comforting arm around her. "It all happened so fast," she said.

Not fast enough to suit him. Unfortunately.

"We got to go back to the house and empty it of the school supplies and such."

"Where will we have the school now? What will happen to it?" Her voice rang out in pain—as if she could barely speak after having been punched in the abdomen.

"Some of the stuff will fit in the smithy." Isaac offered up. It was the most he had said in a week's time. He knew how Pauline felt about the school.

"That's right. Folks got sheds, and a room behind the church. We'll make it work."

Isaac let go of Mandy, and Virgil put his arm around her. As they approached the front door, they encountered the Milford Four, as he started calling them. He tried to steer his wife and daughter away from them, but March, not understanding the situation, ran up to Lucy and hugged her.

Lucy patted his daughter's back, and Virgil took his arm from his wife so that he could step forward to peel March away from the woman. "Excuse us. We'll just be going back now."

Robert Lakey put his hands in his pockets. "Well, Stew. I'm awful sorry. I was afraid it would turn out like this from the beginning, you know."

Mandy flashed that beautiful smile of hers at her old school chum and in the moment, he hated Robert Lakey to the marrow of his soul.

"We'll make a way. My husband said so."

Had he said exactly that? *Dear God. Give me strength to silence myself instead of focusing on silencing others.*

Lucy stepped forward. "Something will work out for the school. Jack says that there must be a school."

"She's right. Even if I help build it or we get funds. Milford will have a schoolhouse." Jack nodded, Clara on his arm, looking very bored.

"What about the children of Crumpton? That's what Mrs. Milford wanted, for them to be educated too."

"Lord Almighty." Clara whipped out a pretty fan from her pocket and began to protect herself in the steamy May day. "Will people ever cease to tell us about what darling Mother wanted?"

Now Mrs. Milford was darling Mama. You had to love that.

Now he spoke. "It was what she said on her deathbed. Mandy was there to hear it, as was I."

Silence fell among them. It didn't make him feel good to silence that Milford woman, but he wasn't going to let her act as if Mandy was some kind of liar, because she had heard those sacred words.

He moved his family to the door. "Excuse us. The sooner we get back, the sooner we can empty out the house for you all."

Jack moved to him. "Let's not be too hasty. Those supplies are necessary to get the school going again. The house has enough space to let the things be stored in a room there until we can figure out where to build a new school that would have suited Mrs. Milford's purposes."

"A splendid idea, Jack!" Lakey chirped.

Virgil rearranged his features so he didn't frown at Lakey's phony cheer. How did Mandy stand going to school with him?

"Why. That's very kind of you, Mr. Kirchner."

"Part of my duties, Mrs. Smithson. The court case is one thing, the school another. The Milford women have the next generation to be provided for, but there must be a school. Mrs. Milford wanted it and so does the Freedman's Bureau. You've done some great work as a start here, and we'll help you to carry it on."

"Goodness, this sun is going to bake me until I'm as black as a darkie." Clara pulled a parasol out of her little bag and put it up. "Lucy don't you have anything to cover yourself? You'll be as dark as a field hand with all of your blond hair."

He didn't trust Lucy, but she did look at Clara as if she would like to take the parasol, close it up, and tap it upside her dark brown curls. Might have been fun if she did.

"Jack is right, Amanda," Lucy said. "I want to help. I'm just learning, but it's been mighty fine to have something to do instead of sitting around all day. Your March, she's so bright, I just know she'll do great things for her race one day. Why her singing voice alone is a marvel, and she has so many other talents. Mother had good feelings for the child, and we would want her and her kind to have a better future."

"I appreciate those words, Mrs. Milford. Thank you." Mandy fairly glowed on his arm.

"We'll be leaving for Atlanta soon. Don't have much time to get these things together." Virgil put in.

"Oh, please don't worry, Mayor. Why don't we gather over it later? We can get the help of the people to store the supplies and to put the house back to rights."

The stony look on Isaac's face struck him. The last thing his friend would want would be another gathering on the town green, and it looked as if things were headed that way. "That would be fine. We'll arrange for something in the front of the house."

The area in front of the Milford house, on the other side of the railroad tracks, stood far away from the town square and away from the unpleasant memories of what happened when they last gathered there.

"Will that do, Mandy?" He grasped his wife's hand in his.

"It will. Thank you, husband."

He turned to face Isaac again to seek his silent approval as deputy mayor, but his friend's eyes were on Tom Dailey as he rode through the town on his horse heading toward his store. The look in Isaac's eyes would light the smithy by itself, and a cold hand closed over Virgil's heart. He clapped a hand on Isaac's shoulder to bring him out of his reverie of hate. "What do you think, Deputy Mayor?"

"Sound fine to me."

"Wonderful. Best get on home."

Robert reached toward his wife . . . to do what? Virgil quickly moved her out of his pathway.

"Stew. Don't worry. It'll be all right in the end. Better and safer for you, you know. Get some rest now."

Lucy drew him back toward her with a gloved hand, but clearly, she didn't mind Robert approaching his wife. Very strange.

They got on the bandbox of the wagon and rode off, in another direction away from the carriage and Charles the Milford flunky.

"Isaac. You got to promise me while you got March that you are not trying to take on Tom Dailey by yourself."

“How do you know they ain’t trying to look for me, knowing I be mad at what they did to my wife?”

Of course, March’s little ears were all into the conversation. “I’m telling you now. Leave it alone. Let God care for it.”

“As he cared for Pauline?” Isaac tossed off.

“Vengeance is mine, saith the Lord. Time will tell.” He slapped Pie’s reins to get them going that much faster ahead of the carriage to Milford. Looking back, he couldn’t tell if they had left yet or not. He slowed down.

“Hmph. Like you felt when them Milfords killed Sally dead, same as if a gun shot her, but slow instead?”

“I was in a very dark place and time. So are you just now.”

“Dark enough, I don’t care what happens.”

Virgil pulled up the reins to stop the wagon and turned to his pretty wife next to him. “Wife, you mind switching up with Isaac? We have some man talk to complete now.”

Virgil helped his Mandy down and into the back of the empty wagonload with March while Isaac climbed up next to him. Virgil started the horses again. “Now you look here. We all care about you. Don’t want nothing to happen to you. Or March for that matter. You don’t show control, what you think them nightriders might do to get a hold of a young one like her?”

Even as he spoke the words, he wanted to be sick in the road at his sweet March meeting such a fate. But he knew he had to use those words to reach his friend. He would not be able to leave for Atlanta otherwise.

“You know I protect March with my very life if I had to.”

"I know, but you need to stop talking about not caring or dying or some other such nonsense. You her uncle and you got to be here to protect her. Understand?"

"Fine. I understand."

Pie was no match for Charles and the Milford horses that pranced on past them on the post road, letting the Milfords win again. Easily.

It would be the last time he would let that happen.

A few hours later they all changed into old clothes to help vacate the school and have a fish fry for dinner together to celebrate the moving of the school elsewhere. It would always be the school to her. Amanda couldn't look at the Milford house any other way. If she did, it would be the place where poor Sally, and even, long, long ago, her own mother, were tortured in their work as Mrs. Milford's chambermaids. She would have to see it as the place where Mrs. Milford sold Sally and used the money made in the sales to improve the house and to make it nicer for herself.

Calling it the school saved it from all of that bad history, and brought it back to a place of good, where Baxters could go to school in comfort, instead of the sweltering heat of the first schoolhouse—or freezing in the wintertime.

Now, the big white behemoth would be facing them without that revision of its history. And where would they be able to have the school anyway?

She started out by cleaning the dust in the parlor while men moved desks and furniture into the room that used to be Mr. Milford's office and library. Calla came to her.

"You let me do that. You go on and help with the fish fry."

"Are you sure? I want to help."

"Want you in good condition for the new school, Amanda. Wherever it will be."

She lowered her head.

"I see you. Looking disappointed." Calla guided her out to the front yards, where two vast iron pots fashioned by her husband were filled with precious hot lard, ready to receive the fish the Baxter cousins would catch. "You get that look on your face sometimes like your mother. I can tell."

"You can?" Something gripped at Amanda's middle. There were not many people in this world who could tell her about the woman who gave birth to her and with whom she shared a name—her middle one. Her father could have told her, but he chose not to. Calla's mention startled her, but something about discussing her mother warmed her.

"Yes. You both get eyebrows meeting in the middle of your forehead. Look like a tent on your face. That's what she did too, had to come to work up in there. She hated it. I was made for that kind of work, so when she get away, it fell on me to do, and I did it for a long, long time."

"And you handed it over to Sally."

"Yes. I got too slow for her. Wanted a younger Baxter, so it was Sally."

Amanda turned to Calla and clasped her hand. "I'm sorry. I didn't mean to make you talk about it."

Calla looked startled. "Why shouldn't I talk about it?"

"The bad old times. Virgil says not to talk about them."

"I'm not him. I think it's good to talk on it. More that we do, less chance we have of going back there. I did what I did to take care of my family, but I'm not never going to be no one's doormat again. That's why, when some of these men say their way or not, I take *not.* It's okay to have some fun tussling around with a man, but no more."

"You know that's fornication? Don't tell Virgil."

"Forny what? Lord, your husband is the biggest pain in the behind. We love him to pieces, but you need to be taking him to Atlanta so we can do what we need to do. Take him right on out of here."

A chill came over Amanda. "Is that why folk vote for him?"

Calla nodded her head. "Partly. He a good man, but he can be mighty stuck on himself at times."

"Well, now, that's not fair. He has a lot on his mind."

Her aunt's eyes softened as she looked at her, arranging some of the knifing tools on the table. "You loves him don't you? That's wonderful. You best hold on to that. It's rare. I had that with my man afore he died. Your mama with that Lawrence man what come to get her. You and your husband. Hold on fast to that. God gave you it to see you through."

"Yes, ma'am."

Calla pointed out to the yard in front of her. "He ain't all bad. Look. He bringing the boys back with fish for you to start cleaning. I'll go back inside and dust."

Virgil came up to her with a full string of wet, smelly trout. Amanda readied her knife, knowing just what to do with it.

"You happy today, wife?"

"It's enough."

"Don't worry about the school. We'll make it right."

"I'll be praying on that, husband."

"You think the church would work for the meantime?"

Well, the church was better than nowhere right now, but it wasn't a real place. It was only one room, so that the older students didn't have a place to learn their lessons as they did now. The older ones would be inconvenienced and have to wait a while until they had a real school.

She tried not to let the pungent fish smell reach her in the nose, but she couldn't help it. Such a strong smell.

CHAPTER SIXTEEN

Even though they had decided to wait until Saturday to leave, her stomach hurt her as Virgil drove the wagon farther from their home in Milford, the one that she had left her heart behind in, the brick house that was their home. She hoped she wasn't getting sick again, as they ventured out on their honeymoon. She hadn't left her heart behind. Her husband was her heart.

Still, March slept while they left before dawn to get a good start on the road. They had said their goodbyes before, but she would still wake up without them in the house, her Uncle Isaac sleeping in the bedroom next to her. She had promised not to abandon her.

Something about that didn't seem fair.

"You feel strange going on a honeymoon with me?"

"It's about time. I guess."

"I would say. I had thoughts of you coming to the state capital with me when I went to take the mayor papers to Milledgeville, but Mrs. Milford didn't think it was such a good idea."

She wrapped her shawl around her to guard against the late spring chill of the morning. “Why not?”

“Had to be about business. And for once that old dragon was right.”

She shook her head. “She was crazy about you.”

She didn’t expect him to answer. He always got very quiet on the subject of his former life. One day, she hoped, he would trust her enough to talk to her about the bad times. But no one, except Calla, ever wanted to talk about those times. She supposed she couldn’t blame them.

Bright pink cracked through the trees, signaling the dawn of the new day. By dinner time, they would be in Atlanta. They would go visit Henry’s church in the morning and have a few days to themselves, before Virgil had to combine business with pleasure and see to setting up his offices and work space in the old City Hall where the new state legislature would meet while they confirmed the move of the state capital, and went about the business of building a new one.

Amanda didn’t mind. It was a whole new start for the entire country, for her formerly enslaved brethren and sisters, and it thrilled her to be a part of it.

I might have been up in Ohio as some old maid schoolteacher.

She knew that wasn’t true though. Her father, having died just days after her graduation, seemed to want her away from Ohio. Once slavery came to an end, her father had insisted when she graduated that they move operations to the south—Milford, Georgia—to help. And she always wanted to know why.

“I stayed down there a few weeks a long time ago.” Her father had told her. “There’s work to be done there.”

From her young frame of mind, she wanted to know how he knew that. But she didn't ask him. She only asked, "Why there?"

"A lot of work to do." Lawrence Stewart seemed lost in his thoughts whenever she asked him, and he gave her the same answer all of the time.

It was true. Thinking of what her father wanted gave her the warm, wrapped-up blanket satisfaction of being where God and her father wanted her to be. Protected by a man, but doing the Lord's work just the same.

"Lots of folk thought I serviced her."

Her husband's words echoed through the woods in the trees on the Old Toll Road. They hit her with a pang, because he sounded hurt.

"Who thought that?" Her shawl went around her even tighter. "How could they?"

Virgil gave a half smile. "Lots of folk do just about anything to get to freedom."

Amanda shuddered and gripped her fingers to try to warm them from the early spring chill. "Who accused you?"

"Well, you know old Franklin wasn't too fond of me. Her sons. Both of them. Some of the Baxters. Why they didn't want Sally to have nothing to do with me. Thought I was her personal attendant."

She knew why he didn't want to use another word. It was an ugly word.

"That's awful. Anyone who knows you knows you have a high moral character."

"Well, Mandy. That was part of what was bad about them bad times. Wasn't nothing about morality. Only reason there wasn't a whole lot of half-Milford half-

Baxter brats running around, was because them Milford men were sore afraid of Millie."

"But that didn't preclude her from trying to get you to pay her some attention."

A frown tugged at the corners of his half smile, pulling it down into his beard. "No."

"So what did you do?"

"What could a preacher do? I talked to her about Joseph and Potiphar's wife. And she was telling me about what happened to old Joseph, how he got thrown down into the prison. I told her that was a trial he had to endure, and the Lord ended up making him most high."

"Thank goodness."

"Yes. She threatened me with everything that she could, but I still insisted I had a right to my own person. I knew God would protect me from her evil intentions. And he did. She never approached me like that again."

"But made you leave once you married Sally. That wasn't right."

"More of that kind of thing like she didn't want Sally to have me if she couldn't. She was a mean, selfish woman."

Amanda reflected on the former plantation mistress she had known for a few months, and decided he was right. She felt for Lucy and Clara who must shepherd the Milford interests in her name.

She and Virgil had only two years doing it, and they had done relatively well, but it might be time for a new regime in place.

"I'm sorry, husband. Still, I'm your wife. If you want to tell me about those times, you should. There should be nothing between us."

Her husband's handsome jaw set on edge "Some things, what you don't know, is for your protection, Mandy. Remember, I'm thinking always of what protects you and March." He lifted his arm to wrap it around her.

Instantly, the shawl that she wore was too much of an extra layer to be between him and her.

So she slipped the shawl down, and it landed with a soft thud on their valises in the back of the wagon, and he guided Pie with one hand.

They continued on to Atlanta in a slow, but determined way, holding onto each other in the breaking dawn of the day, readying for the new future that was to come to them both.

Hope burned a small fire in her belly and dissolved her need for breakfast.

One of Atlanta's newest, and most exclusive hotels had been built down the street from the City Hall. It would have been the perfect place to take a bride on a honeymoon.

But they could not stay there.

He did point out to her the dilapidated wooden structure that was the old City Hall. One of the few buildings Sherman and his boys had left standing. That was where the new Georgia government was supposed to work from. "Better than what they left in Milledgeville," Virgil intoned as they moved onto the northern side of town, where the Turners lived. The day was beginning to come to a close, and soon, the streets would be filled with frolicking people who wanted to imbibe alcohol and have something to say to a smartly dressed Negro couple. No. Better to be moving on.

Just as the darkness fell, Virgil pulled up to the Turner house. They were just about to sit to table, and he was glad of it, because he was starved. Tunis wasn't there, but the regular boarders really straightened up when they saw Mandy come to table and put on their best manners. Well, he knew from his brief knowledge of her that Mrs. Turner would run a tight ship as it was.

When they lifted their heads from prayer, Henry grinned at him. "Mother, I'll have you to know that these two are on their honeymoon."

"Really? Well, they will get extra special treatment then and not be disturbed."

"We were married in '66, but this is the first time we've been on a trip intentionally together." Mandy informed her, removing her bonnet.

"Isn't that beautiful? And Virgil told us how you met and married, but maybe our boarders would like to hear it?"

He watched Mandy very carefully to make sure she ate most of her potatoes, beans, slice of ham and square of cornbread. The helper girl made sure her glass was filled with milk, then teawater. The boarders, captivated by his wife, watched her most of the meal. He didn't mind, and told the story as everyone ate of their vanilla custard. When he finished the story he said, "That brings us to today, right Mrs. Smithson?"

"Just about. Thank you, husband." She let her spoon slip into the wiggling custard, and he smiled at her, wanting to hold her hand.

Mrs. Turner wiped at the corners of her eyes with a towel. "I love a good love story."

One of the boarders muttered as he picked up his square of custard, full bore on his spoon and let it slide down his throat. "What did you say, Arnold?"

"Can't hardly get any luckier than that. Some fellows get all the luck."

He moved his attention to the young man at the end of the table and gave what he hoped was a friendly smile. "God sees to all of our needs in time. I prayed that would happen with my wife, once I knew her coming to Milford was one of the best things that ever happened to me. I'm praying the same when we're seated in legislature."

Henry pulled his chair back from the table, having consumed his small slice of custard long before. Virgil ate it quickly, to make a show of being polite, but it was nothing like Amanda's.

"We sure got to pray on it, Brother. Signs aren't looking too promising that they will seat us. They saying the election wasn't legal."

"What do we keep coming up here for? I expect to be seated." Virgil wiped his lips with his napkin, impatient.

"You will. But best be believed that it's going to take another fight." Turner looked around to see if there were any other slices of custard going uneaten. Still there was plenty of food. Not that tasty, but it was hot and people were treated with respect here and at Hampshire's. But, he wasn't taking Mandy over there—the widow Hampshire fixed her eyes on him like he was the last biscuit left on the table at a boarding house, and Mandy should not have to deal with some shifty-eyed woman, hungry for her man.

"I'm sorry to hear that the South cannot accept the loss of the war." Mandy said, folding her hands in her lap.

All around the table, the men fell quiet. One man started to slurp on his custard, so that the only sound in the room was a wet slapping sound. Guess it was better than no dessert.

"Don't mean to offend you, Mrs. Smithson. But for us folk, it's a case of the devil and the deep blue sea."

"Because?"

"Well, Mandy, while the Union folks allowed for things to get moving into place some, they still aren't crazy about the whole idea of former slaves in the government."

"No, not at all." Henry was finally resigned his wife would serve him no more custard, and he pushed his plate away. Mrs. Turner cut him a satisfied gaze and picked up his plate to begin to stack with the others. Marriage was a contest in a lot of ways, for sure. That was something he learned over the past almost two years. And not even then, if you counted the time he was away for the Constitutional Convention.

"We had an election. Jack Kirchner certified it. That should be enough for everyone." Mandy pushed back the plate on the table in some distress.

"Well, whether the Union soldiers and the Freedman's Bureau work together or not is another thing altogether, Mrs. Smithson." Henry informed her with that loose smile of his.

Mandy's dimples popped out as they did when her face was all frowned up. "I don't understand all of this. First people say there is a government. Now there is word that it won't hold up. What were you gone for five months for?"

"There had to be a constitution so that there would be a government and a way for Georgia to be sworn back into the Union." Turner pulled out his pipe and started to light it up, a signal for many men to do the same. Virgil did not take tobacco, but he would stay to hear the rest of this important talk.

"Now that's happened, and they are trying to abandon the ones that got them there?" Mandy's face scrunched up.

His wife was so smart. "Yes, Mandy." He took up her dainty hand, holding it to make sure it was warm.

"How long have people known about this?"

Now here was the bad part. "Been knowing ever since the Convention was on."

She turned to him. "You mean, you knew all this time that there was a possibility that you wouldn't be seated?

He nodded. There was nothing else to say, and now the sound of the room permeated with thick, blue, smoke. She really should leave, but she remained firmly seated in her chair. He could tell she was disturbed by how straight her back was.

"Well, Mrs. Smithson. Sometimes these things take time. Your husband and several of the men here, along with myself—we have jobs to do. And if it comes to seeing progress for the formerly enslaved among us, it may require a sacrifice. One that may seem mighty hard to pay."

Henry moved his considerable bulk to move behind Mandy's chair and stood behind it, hands on it, ready to pull it out.

But Mandy stayed firm in the chair. "So much of a sacrifice. The school. Our baby. Everything between us. What else will this new government require?"

Her question echoed in the room as the moist lips of the men all around his wife quieted into a practice of contemplation.

To tell the truth, he himself did not know.

So she finally did what she was supposed to and excused herself. A hole opened in his heart as her warmth moved from his side.

In short order, so did Mrs. Turner and the helper girl, to clear dishes.

Once all of the women left the room, Henry said, "Heh, I tell you that's why women shouldn't be involved in politics. So emotional."

Mandy had every reason to be angry with him that he should keep such information to himself. "My wife is college educated, more than a lot of men at this table. She'd be a better candidate than many here, and I would include myself. It was great fortune for me that she was born a woman, but maybe it's worse for her."

"And did you tell her about bringing her school up here?"

"It's not as easy as all of that. Those people down there are her family. She wants a change in the Baxter family, and she has it in her mind that she's the one to make the change."

"Maybe he ain't so lucky after all." Arnold said from the other end of the table and some snorted in laughter with him.

"I am," Virgil spoke aloud. "And my Mandy is someone who will make change. It's important that these young ones come up learning how to read and write. She taught me, and I'm not ashamed to say it. She could be teaching some of you."

He stood up to see several of the men averting their eyes. He knew it. Henry and Tunis were literate men, but there were others, too many who were to be part of the new government who weren't. "Doubtless, she would have her hands full with a number here at the table here, if I were to let her. Excuse me."

He pushed the chair into the table and strode out the room. Snatches of laughter and murmurs of, "Maybe she should start a school here," followed him. *Humph.* They weren't worth the time of his wife.

He walked through the front door of the house onto the porch, expecting to see Mandy taking the cool of the evening out there, but she wasn't there. Instead, he heard snatches of female laughter and companionship from the kitchen where she was talking with Mrs. Turner and her helper. "We can get started in the morning, Matilda. Why don't they have any schools here?"

"They don't see no need for us to have none."

"And your sisters and brothers have no school as well?"

"Nome. We all got to work to help our house."

"We'll work on this. I have to know when my husband starts his work, and then I can begin my work. And I will."

Virgil's heart lightened. Maybe she understood. Maybe she would be willing to come to Atlanta and have the school here. He took in a whiff of the air and immediately regretted it. The smell of unwashed bodies, sewage and spoiled food nearly knocked him over. No

Milford, this place. He certainly would miss the fresh country air. But, new times were coming and new ways had to be made.

He stayed out there on the porch and spoke cordially to some of the men who had wandered out, asking about his wife's intentions and how long they would be in Atlanta. While he was on that porch, he had figured out a place where they could live, and even a place in a neighborhood called Summerville, where Mandy might be able to have a school very inexpensively. God was looking out for them, seeking to make all of their plans and dreams come true.

So he went into their attic bedroom that night and he laid down on sheets that were crisp and fresh for the newlywed couple. He reached for her, but Mandy turned her back on him and not in a way where he could snuggle up to her.

He lay on his back for most of the night. He would not turn from her as she did him. *Please God. There has to be a way to work this out.*

Still, all he could think of was the sacrifice.

And he knew it wasn't fair to her.

CHAPTER SEVENTEEN

Her dreams were haunted with all of the things she wanted to say to her husband.

So much so, she had to convince herself that she was dreaming, not screaming at her husband awake.

So when he turned over and he fluttered his eyelashes up to show he was awake, she pounced.

"How could you not tell me?"

"Mandy. I'm just trying to thank God to allow me to greet the day. May I do that, wife?"

"Of course," she replied sweetly and adjusted the scarf wrapped around her braids. "I would not dream of stopping you from communing with God."

His Adam's apple moved, cutting a swath through his neck. "Would you like to join me?"

"Yes."

They clasped hands, facing each other, while Virgil prayed. "Dear Lord, please let us lean on you for understanding and love. Let us not ask others for clarity, we seek only you to know how the loved ones in our lives would have us know the true motives and situations of our hearts. Be close to us at this time that we need you, in the name of your son who died on the cross to cover our sins. Amen."

They opened their eyes to face one another.

"That's a powerful lot of praying you doing, just to thank the Almighty to get up in the morning."

"Wife, I know you're upset with me. I need all the help I can get."

She squeezed his hand and let it go, but he rested it on her hip. *Uh oh.* "We've church this morning. See if Henry is a better preacher than you."

"I know what we got to do. We also on our honeymoon."

"We'll be late to breakfast."

"I don't care nothing for breakfast if you haven't made it." He moved in on her neck and started laying some small kisses along her neckline.

"We don't want to offend Mrs. Turner."

Virgil whispered in her ear. "Ain't none of my affair if the woman can't cook. If it wasn't our honeymoon, you should get in the kitchen and show her a thing or two. Poor men would be starving up in here."

"It's a nice enough boarding house," she managed to get out as Virgil kept tracing kisses down the length of her body causing her to squirm up against him. "If you stay here while you are in Atlanta, then you won't starve and now I know that."

"Wife." Virgil whispered softly into her ear. "You wanting me up here doing the work of the people and you wouldn't be by my side? You know I need you."

His hand snaked up the side of her leg taking some of her long nightgown with him.

"I need you too. I would miss you dreadfully, husband."

"No need for us to be separated. We can all come here together. Just for a few years."

A few years. A long time. How could she leave behind the caresses and cares of her husband, in exchange for the love of her family and Pauline . . .

Except Pauline wasn't there anymore. All the emotions that her husband stirred in her, and she clung to him, tired of her brain working so hard, and let her heart decide. What would Isaac give to be able to do this with Pauline right now? How ungrateful she would be if she didn't partake of what God wanted for them to do—right now.

For just the second time since all of the pain and loss, the good feelings she knew were possible, came back to her for a painfully short time as she stroked the back of his neck. She was reminded of everything that was possible between them.

So when she had returned to her own mind, she didn't realize Virgil's hand covered her mouth.

Pulling his body away from her, he took his hand from her mouth extremely slowly, so slowly that she grabbed his wrist.

"What was that for?" an irritated feeling bubbled up inside of her.

"We don't need the whole boarding house to know what we up to, Mandy."

"Ha! You were the one who started all of this."

"I know, but really, wife." He reclaimed his hand with a smile. "You'll need to control yourself more."

She threw a pillow after him, and he ducked very precisely, having extremely honed instincts at avoiding all types of missiles.

It was just another way that he was able to prove he was exceptional, and she wiggled in frustration to get off the bed to see if Mrs. Turner had held any of her breakfast back for them.

"Why, certainly." Mrs. Turner pulled a cloth from the plates of runny eggs and lumpy oatmeal she had made. "I wouldn't dare deprive a honeymooning couple of their food. You all need to keep up your strength."

Thankfully the table had emptied of the boarders by the time they came downstairs, Amanda leading the way and apologizing.

"This was so kind of you." She swallowed her gorge. "I could have made something."

"No. That's not the way to be. Besides, Henry just getting down here himself. Mornings when he got to preach, I let him sleep in."

When Mrs. Turner spoke, Henry McNeal Turner appeared in the doorway, smiling extra broadly at Virgil. "Morning to you all. Wonderful day in the Lord. isn't it?"

"It is." Virgil started upon the hateful task of scooping up the food to eat. Her husband was so incredibly modest; Amanda knew he suffered to have other people know what they had been up to in the large attic room.

"My plate, wife." Reverend Turner gestured, and Mrs. Turner came running forward with it and set it down before him, making a production of serving her husband. Amanda set herself before the task of eating every morsel on her plate, knowing that if it had been the month before, she would not have been able to finish it.

"It's a good morning." Reverend Turner tucked into his eggs. "Must have caught a few of those roof rats up above your heads."

"You got roof rats?" Virgil put his fork down with haste.

"Oh, they up above you. Not likely to break on through. If you hear some scratching. That's usually them. Today though, I heard them screaming. Must have caught a couple in my traps."

She watched as Virgil picked up his fork went to work on the runny eggs, now that he had finished chewing on his oatmeal.

"Henry." Mrs. Turner sat down in her spot at the end of the table with a coffee pot at her right hand.

"Yes, dear. I'm eating my breakfast."

"Be sure you do."

Mrs. Turner turned to her. "You make sure to let me know if you want more. You have to keep your strength up you know."

"Yes, ma'am." Amanda pondered the impossible task in front of her in eating just what was in front of her. Keep her strength up for what? Keeping up a school everyone seemed to want her to shut down. Starting another? A baby? Her life wanted to split off into so many forks, it was hard to know which road to take.

Dear Lord. Help me to know how to decide what is best for us. For me. For Virgil. For March. For Milford College. For the future. Amen.

She felt instantly better in relieving her heart to her Lord. Except, the eggs and oatmeal had not disappeared from her plate.

Maybe there were other things to pray for. She applied herself to clearing her plate, knowing there were sacrifices ahead. That's what she needed strength for.

"He can't hold a candle to you, and you know it." Mandy stuffed her hand into the crook of his arm as they took a late afternoon walk away from the boarding house. They wanted to take Pie and the wagon, but Henry told them the city streets were too crowded for a big old wagon.

"Would be better to rent a carriage or walk." Henry told them. "Too hard getting around otherwise."

So they walked, rather than waste the money on a fancy carriage. In the Summerhill part of Atlanta, there were places to eat, and they opted to eat in a nice family restaurant where they were welcome, instead of returning to the boarding house where Mrs. Turner had laid out a cold spread, out all day.

"That was a meal more like I am used to." He rubbed his front when he had finished eating the beefsteak.

"She's not used to cooking for a bunch of folks. That's all."

"I never thought of it that way."

"A boarding house is a good business for a woman to have in Atlanta now. People are coming in, city's starting to grow again, new buildings being built. Men who are here need home-cooked meals and clean places to live." Mandy looked over her shoulder picking up her napkin to fold it.

"Would you do it?"

"I lived for so many years in boarding houses. I never thought I would live in one again." His wife fiddled with the edge of her napkin, and a pang struck him at her distress. What kind of life had Lawrence Stewart given to his daughter? She didn't talk much about it—just as he didn't talk much about the old days, but he knew where this had come from. As educated as his wife was, her excellent cooking skills made no sense at all, unless you took into account the haphazard way that her father brought her up.

"I don't mind staying in one for temporary." She fixed him with her lovely eyes, and he held up a hand to get a check. And a slice of pie.

"Peach," he told the serving woman. "What will you have, wife?"

"Nothing, thank you."

"I knew what you meant. If we came here, it would be in a house."

She fell silent. This was one of the reasons they walked a nice distance from the Turner home, to see what the Summerhill neighborhood was like. It was nice enough with wooden houses built, and one or two new stone built churches being built. Everywhere they walked, they could see prosperous black couples walking up and down the streets. People who looked like them.

"Is the old City Hall close enough?" she asked as he paid the check.

"It's on the way back."

"Great." The waitress bought them the check and him a generous slice of peach pie. "I'll get started on this and we'll walk out there together."

"Please bring another fork." Mandy told the waitress, and she pulled another set up from an apron pocket, grinning, and handed it to Amanda.

"I asked you if you wanted to order something, wife."

"I know. I just want a few forkfuls is all."

That fork went in and out of his pie more times than he might like to count for both of them. Mandy wiped her beautiful little mouth with a napkin. "Thank you for the tastes, wife."

"Everyone's got to make a sacrifice." She stood up in her purple sprigged dress and pulled her shawl closer on her.

Sometimes, that scamp Mandy was just too smart for her own good.

The City Hall was quite the hike from Summerhill, but fortunately, it wasn't too far from the Turner house. The building didn't impress her much. She had thought her shoes fit her well, but she had some other ideas by the time Virgil pointed out a large beige sandstone building ahead of them, being built up. "There's the Opera House."

"It's all stone."

"Might be a place to think more about meeting. That old City Hall building is way too small."

"Let's look at it."

He laid a hand on her hand, and they approached going into the building together when several officers approached them on horseback.

"Hey, you. Where're you going?"

Virgil turned around to face the officers and her heart stopped. What could they have possibly done? They were just taking a walk around Atlanta, trying to see the sights if there were any to be seen, but Atlanta was too new yet to offer much.

Her husband squeezed her hand. "I'm a newly elected state representative. Just wanted to show the wife the new Opera House."

"What's your name?"

This time she squeezed his hand.

"I'm Virgil Smithson and this is my wife, Amanda. And who might you gentlemen be?"

One of the police officers pulled something out of his vest pocket and looked down at it, consulting with another officer. She opened her mouth to ask a question, her husband's hold on her hand was a vice grip. She knew he would never hurt her in a million years. His eyes were alit with a fire she did not understand.

Be quiet this time.

Well, all right then. She telegraphed back to him.

Still, why were these police officers keeping them here?

Her desire to ask a question, the foundation of her education and upbringing from Lawrence Stewart, and her newly born desire to be a good wife, born less than two years ago, warred with each other.

"He's the one we are looking for."

And the long-held desire won out. "What do you mean?" The question burst forth from her lips like a horse from the gate.

Virgil let go of her hand and wrapped an arm around her shoulders and pulled her to him, almost stretching himself across her like a shield.

"Pastor Turner wants you to get back to his house right away. Says there's a message there for you."

Relief slipped from her body, leaving it liquid jelly.

"Thank you, gentlemen. If you will excuse us." Virgil turned, taking her by the hand again, and they walked quickly in the direction of the boarding house.

"Whew. Thank goodness. They just wanted to give us a message."

Her husband said nothing, but picked up his pace just a bit, making it just that much harder for her to keep up with him.

"A message. From home? We've only been here a day and half. Could it be from home?" Something unpleasant stirred in her stomach, reminding her of the sickness that she would have when the baby was still inside of her. Sending the police to look out for them? Whatever the news was, it had to be serious to have Henry send the police looking for them. He knew most Negroes wanted nothing to do with law enforcement officials. "Would he send the police for something that was related to state business?"

"No." Virgil stopped suddenly to let a horse and carriage go by in front of them.

Her heart pounded faster from the exercise. And fear.

"Slow down."

"It's just another few streets over."

"These shoes . . . they are killing my feet." Amanda's legs wobbled like a newly born baby animal.

"You might break an ankle in them things."

"That's why I'm saying to slow down, husband. If it is from home, we'll go back and make it all right."

"I feel the devil's hand in this. We need to pray."

"Please do."

Right there on the pine sidewalk of Atlanta, she and her husband joined hands and dipped their heads in obedience to Him. "We are your humble children, Lord, giving up all in sacrifice to you. We only want to do your will. So whatever this is that awaits us, please, give us the strength and courage that we need to fight it. Help us Lord, and protect the ones that we love. In your name, Amen."

When he lifted his head, Virgil was off, practically running and Amanda joined him as best as she could.

When they reached the front porch of the house, a number of the boarders were outside, relaxing, and smoking their pipes. Someone called out to Henry that they had arrived and he came out on the porch with a stern look on his face.

Was this how it felt to stand before God on Judgment Day? To have your heart nearly explode, to pray that whatever might come their way, they would handle it?

"March is missing."

"Missing? What does the message say?"

"It's from Brother Isaac, the gentleman that you introduced us to." Henry held out the message and Virgil grabbed it, none too gently and gave it to Amanda.

He could read now, but she suspected he didn't want to at this moment.

So it was up to her.

Tears blurred her sight and she used the back of her hand to read the message that had come from Crumpton by telegraph.

March gone. Most of the night. Sending out a search party in the morning. Praying for her safety. Some saying. Kidnapped.

“Oh, Virgil. Isaac thinks she’s been kidnapped.”

He took up the piece of paper from her to examine it himself and waved it in the air. “March is a child of the woods. She stay out there most days by herself if we let her. Nobody looking to take her.” The edge of his jaw was an exact square.

“We’ve got to get back as soon as possible.” Amanda didn’t even realize Mrs. Turner had come out of the house to hold her shoulders. Mrs. Turner smelled like vanilla, and she was grateful someone could hold onto her. It wasn’t her husband. He bristled all over, like a porcupine—and angry.

“Who would take March?”

The question lingered around, so many frightening possibilities swirling in her mind at who might want to harm their darling child.

“Brother.” Henry Turner stepped forward and laid a hand on Virgil’s shoulder. “These are some terrible times. White man don’t want us to make any moves forward—or have any power. You got to recognize that you have power now. Taking March and hiding her some place is a way to get your sure enough attention.”

“He’s right, Virgil.” Amanda clasped her hands.

So in a way, March’s disappearance from the face of the earth was her fault. She had encouraged him to run for office and to be a leader for his people, and here was the outcome. Uncertainty in the legality of office, and March gone, just like Pauline, just like her baby.

Dear God, she prayed, *when will the sacrifices stop?*

CHAPTER EIGHTEEN

When they heard that the train wouldn't come for six more hours, Virgil shook his head. "We can get home before then."

Pie carried them both on her back without complaint. So, with just the minimum clothes on, leaving the wagon and everything behind them, they rode swiftly through the Georgia early evening, knowing that when they arrived in Milford, they would arrive in complete darkness.

Would they be able to look for March then? In the darkness?

Her husband's arms surrounded her as they both rode on the horse, pushing her poor Pie further than she ought to be. Somehow though, through the tension in their legs and thighs, somehow, Pie knew they had to get home fast. So she bore her burden with strength. A real lesson to her.

The May night warmed them both, so they weren't cold, but there was ice in Amanda's heart. Where could March be? As if she said it, or maybe she did, Virgil answered her heart. "Isaac was new to taking care of her—Pauline knew about all of her wanderings and hiding places. She's somewhere in one of them, and when we get there, we'll find her."

"It just doesn't seem likely that someone would take her because they don't like you being in office."

Even as Amanda said it out loud, the thought was entirely plausible.

"I shouldn't have left her with Isaac. He wasn't being careful because of Pauline. I thought they might be comfort for one another, but he wasn't being watchful."

"Oh, husband, I think you had the exact right feeling in your heart. It's just . . . something went horribly wrong, and we'll find out what it is."

"No matter what we find when we get back home, I'm going to make this all up to both of you."

She grasped at Pie's mane to stave off sleep. "I've been thinking about it too. It's my fault. I've put more expectations on us. I'm going to be wherever you are. In Atlanta, if I have to. I don't want to be without my family. Not anymore."

The tears welled behind her eyes, causing that too familiar pain. Even though Virgil couldn't see her face, he murmured words of comfort into her ear through her braids. Still, she didn't want to cry. They didn't need that now. They needed to be strong just now. For March.

"I don't either, Mandy. We going to make all of this work somehow."

"I didn't mean to put the school before you."

"You didn't, Mandy. I knew what you were doing. You brought so much—light here."

She leaned back, just that little bit against her husband's broad chest and between his smooth, hard biceps, because safety and protection dwelled in the circle of his arms. She just wished March was there too.

"I wanted to do as my father would have me. Knowledge is light."

"I was afraid of that light. You know it. I was a coward before the light I knew the Lord wanted for me. I'm not going to be afraid anymore."

"I don't know what you mean, husband."

"This whole thing, this election. I have to serve my turn, do what I have to do. Sitting around talking to Henry and Tunis, they seem to know more things than I do."

"That's not true, Virgil. You know what you need to serve the people in Milford and Crumpton. That's the way to see it. Not in comparison to Henry and Tunis. Try to think of it that way."

"That makes the most sense. But biggest thing is, I want to be someone who brings opportunity to Milford for March. For you. And for any other child we can have. If that's what you want."

"All I want is March in my arms again."

He squeezed her in his hold. "Me too, Mandy. Go Pie."

Pie went on in the darkness, carrying them through the night; man, woman, and horse, in a posture of cold uncertainty for what would come in the future.

Pie stepped into the edge of Crumpton and Virgil stopped. "Rebecca, Lena and them live here. You might want to get to inside and stay for the night while I push on to Milford, find Isaac and see what they are doing to find her."

"I don't want to go anywhere else."

"I'm going to start searching the woods back here and work my way to Milford."

"You think she can be this far out?"

"I'm not ruling anything out."

They knocked on Lena Stimpson's door. Lena was an older student at her school, and there was a long hesitation before the door opened. Amanda didn't blame them. It didn't pay for anyone to be too forward at who might be knocking at the door when the sun went town. Lena's father George opened the door and they stepped inside. Without a word, Lena's mother Rebecca came forward and gathered Amanda into her arms.

"They looking for her. They doing everything to find her, honey. We wondered when and how you all was getting back."

Her husband George dressed and came back into the front room. "Virgil's a fool, trying to get out there by himself."

Rebecca looked alarmed. "I thought you were staying here."

George pointed to Amanda. "You got the spare gun. Mrs. Mayor here is a good shot. You'll be fine here. I'm afraid whoever got her; they might be trying to draw Virgil into some kind of trap. Best that he get some company."

"Be careful." Rebecca rushed up to her husband and kissed him full on the lips, not caring Amanda was there, sitting at the table. How fortunate Rebecca was to have her husband to kiss. *Dear God, please don't let anything happen to these men.*

Rebecca shut the door quietly after her husband and shushed her children back to bed. "I got some coffee made. Let me pour you some, Teacher."

"Thank you."

"They going to get her. Don't you fret none."

"What if?" The vague thought on the edge of her consciousness formed in her mind. "What if someone took March to do bad to her?"

Rebecca's ice-cold hand gripped hers. "We claiming good in the name of the Lord. Just like you, the good come down here to show our people a new and better way, making a way for my Lena to be a teacher one day like you. We're claiming the good in His name."

"Amen."

"Sip on that coffee. We got to pray in the name of Jesus that our menfolk come back to us safe, and that Miss March comes back from staying out too long. Then we all going to take a turn whipping her little fanny causing us to be so scared."

"You're going to have to wait your turn." Amanda sipped at her coffee, reflecting on how little she had ever punished March. Is that why this was happening to them now?

Things were going to change a great deal, whatever the outcome of this terrible episode in her life and she sipped at the coffee some more to be ready to greet this great change God had in store for them—whatever it was.

He never had a choice in having the children he had.

Picking his way with George trailing behind him on an old Indian trail through the woods, he clutched the mean poor lantern and held it out far in front of him. He remembered how Sally told him she was having March, mere minutes it seemed, after they had jumped over the broom in front of the Milford farmhouse.

He had been so young then, before the War, before he had won his freedom, before death, before anything meaningful. When she had told him, the news made him feel all mixed up inside like taking in a cube of sugar soaked in bitter medicine. What did a baby mean for him? It all seemed so unreal and created somehow. Upshot was, he hadn't been that great about it to Sally either, and they had a fight.

Lord, as of right now, tonight, if you see fit to bless me any further with children, March or her brothers and sisters, I vow I'm going to be glad of it.

He held up the lantern a bit more to see into the darkness. "Nothing over there but the old boathouse for Master Bolton." George said.

"Some of his boys part of the night riders, it might bear checking out."

There was a rustling of some bushes in front of them. It easily could have been an animal at this time of night, but Virgil readied the gun George had loaned to him. "March! March!"

George hushed him. "Don't call out too loud. We don't want any of the whites hearing."

George made a point. There was no need to get those folk tied up in this mess. And honestly, would his little girl be this far away from home? It made no sense.

He had barely known March as a baby, because he was forced to leave home once he bought his freedom, but when he had encountered her again, when she was five, it was like coming upon a tall tree in the woods planted years before. Startling.

"This be miles from you." George intoned. "How could she make it this far—she's just a little thing? Better double back, and try to cover the ground between us and Milford."

"I don't know if that's right. I know Isaac been out that way."

"And that he probably checked the water."

That realization slapped him in the face like a young, green tree branch bent back. He gripped his horse's reins further. Someone ended up gone—that was the first order of business. To check the water.

"See if she went back to Africa. Didn't Titian Baxter?

Virgil's lips tightened. He had been a young man and had been forced to help when one of Sally's brothers, Titian, was found on the edge of an inlet. His bloated body was not a pleasant memory. "Yep. That's not where she going to be. She don't even know anything about Africa."

"She so small though. She might have slipped in the water somehow."

"March swims."

"Sometimes the currents are mighty strong, and she skinny."

He was inclined to turn back around when a light dawned ahead and something drew him to it. "That a cabin up ahead?"

"No. Another boathouse."

"Why is it lit up?"

"Let's go see." George led the way to the place and Virgil tied up Pie, dismounting quickly to see if a lantern in a boathouse could have been someone seeking shelter, some folks trying to find a place to carry on, or something more.

"Heyah! March!"

There was a rustling behind him, and March came into his view, wearing her white dress, but it was all torn and dirty and her hair all over her head.

His knees failed him, and he sank to the ground with a thud and embraced the child. A powerful pressure rose up in him, and he wanted to release his emotions all over her, but he knew he couldn't. March hadn't said a word.

"Are you okay, March? You got half the county looking for you, and your uncle crazy with worry."

"I'm glad you came back to find me, Papa."

"What happened, child?"

"I tried to get back to you all, and the man told me the road to Atlanta. I started to walk, knowing I would get there if I just started out."

"Girl, you supposed to be staying with your Uncle. He taking care of you while we was gone."

"He seem so sad, I thought he thinking about Africa, and I didn't want that to happen. So I tried to find you to tell you."

So much for her not knowing about Africa. His child was always in the grown folks' business.

His desire to shake her went from him, and he picked her up in his arms as if she were five again, completely forgetting she was old and big now. He could still do it, and that was what mattered. He put her on the horse.

"Let's get back to the women, George. I know they be worried."

He wanted to shout halleluiahs to worship the pink dawn that started to break through the thick forest trees and lit the waterway for the day. Made it so much easier to get back.

When they returned, Amanda spotted them, and she came running out, moving faster than she had in weeks. Her arms reached up, hungry to hold March in them. He slipped March to her as his wife cried with gratitude at her safety.

He understood, but March's sense of quiet was still unnerving to him. Of course, a lot of things about March unnerved him. The way she knew things, her singing, her dancing, her way with plants and the dogs. Pauline had told him March was one of God's singular creations, and he should be proud to be her father.

He was, but he always felt relieved, when he looked at her, that she had been too young to know anything of the bad old times.

He hoped.

March was so slight that the three of them on Pie was no big deal, and he refused George's offer of another horse to take them back to Milford. "If we go slow, old Pie will take us home." He explained.

They had wrapped March in an old quilt, and Amanda held her in her arms as if she were a baby, as Pie took the toll road back to Milford.

"I wouldn't have left if Uncle Isaac hadn't kept talking about going back to Africa, but first he had business with Tom Dailey."

"Is that why you were taking the road?"

"Someone had to warn old Tom Dailey about Uncle Isaac's business, and so I went to Crumpton to the store. It's on the way to Atlanta anyhow. I had some money for candy too."

Virgil's teeth set on edge. Those temptations were straight from the devil.

"Did you get your candy?" Mandy asked her.

"I did, and then Tom Dailey started asking me a whole lot of questions about you all, and where you were and was I by myself."

Pie's tread was incredibly slow, almost as if they had stopped. "What happened then?" Mandy gestured to him to be still and quiet. It was almost as if their slowed talk lulled all of them into another state of mind.

"I didn't tell him nothing. It wasn't none of his business where you were. But, when I left the store with my horehound drops, he came up on me on the road and offered to show me a faster way to get to Atlanta. I wanted to find you all, so I went with him."

Dear Lord.

"He got off of the horse and went into the woods, and it started getting dark and it didn't look like it was nowhere on the road to Atlanta, no matter what. He told me we could stay in the boathouse until it got to be light again, and we could go on to Atlanta some more."

He didn't realize it, but he had started to pray under his breath. If Tom Dailey had harmed his child in some way, it was the end of everything. He would have to hang for killing him and that was the end of all of the promise and hope for them all.

"We went to the boathouse, and there was a bed on the boat and he told me to lay down on it, but I didn't feel sleepy and I said I would stay outside."

"That was a good idea." Mandy said in an impossibly light voice.

"He kept trying to get me to come in there, and I said no. I wanted to get away to get back to the Atlanta road I was on and then he stopped calling."

"Why do you think that happened?" How could Mandy be so calm?

"I don't know, Mama. I thought he fell asleep, but then when I went in there to see why, he wasn't moving. I tried to wake him up, but he wasn't moving around—he was like Aunt Pauline in her coffin, silent as the tomb."

Then Pie stopped, and their house loomed before them.

But they didn't go inside.

"He was dead?" Virgil prayed it was true.

"Seem like to me he was. Deader than anything, and I have had plenty of funerals in my life for people and for animal friends. So, I just come outside and tried to find my way back to the Atlanta road and that's where you found me Papa. I was so glad to see you. I prayed to Jesus to let you all come and find me, cause I was scared and you did."

"When were you the most scared, child?"

"When he took me out to that boathouse. He's a nasty, dirty man, like you said, and I know it was his gun what killed Aunt Pauline. But, I wanted to be with you all more than that."

"Did he hurt you?"

A thick hard lump gathered in his throat. *Help me, God; help me to hear what this child has to say.*

"He kept pulling on my arms and stuff, and I said no."

"Just your arms though?"

"Yes. My arms. Then he went in that boathouse to lie down, and he never came out no more."

"Did you tell anyone else he was in there, March?"

"No. I was trying to come out of the woods to find you."

"And you sure he was dead back in there?"

"He wasn't moving. And he smelled. I had to get out of there."

He and Mandy looked at one another. Her dimples had appeared on her face and her cheeks quivered. He set his jaw and just shook his head slightly, to say they would talk about it when they were alone. She seemed to understand, and obey, this time.

Mandy gathered her in her arms. "I'm so glad you are safe back with us, child."

"I am, too."

"And we're always going to be together. As a family." Virgil insisted.

"Really, Papa?"

"Really. I'm promising you that today." Pie went on to the barn—poor horse needed rest. She wanted to be at home. He understood. The sacrifice of his children was too high a price to pay for all of this glory and greatness of the state legislature. Milford was where he belonged, with his family.

But first, they had to find out what had happened to Tom Dailey.

And see if March was responsible in any way.

CHAPTER NINETEEN

Virgil tied Pie up and charged Mandy to take care of the horse.

"We got Isaac's horses. Isaac and me got to go back out."

Mandy cast a look back at the sleeping March, who lay on the red davenport with her dogs surrounding her protectively.

"Please, be careful." She gripped his sleeve.

"I know what I have to do, Mandy." He seemed irritated with her, but she didn't care. He had to hear what it was she had to say.

They stepped out onto their porch and he strapped on his pistol.

She touched him on the arm as she spoke, "If anything happened to you. Anything, after all that has happened, I don't think I . . ."

He gripped her arm in return and stared down into her eyes with his Judgment Day look on his face that secretly thrilled her when she first came to Milford. "We love each other. All of us. Mandy, that love doesn't just go away. It's always here with us. It's in you, and it's in me. You will be fine. The school will go on, and you will too. Promise me."

She didn't realize that tears were slipping down her face until she tasted her own salt. "I can't promise what I don't know. It's all too much."

"Remember God asked a lot of Abram, and he was a man of God who stood strong in the sacrifice. Stand strong."

She couldn't say any more. She didn't want him speechifying at her anymore. She just wanted him to do what he needed to do and come home to her.

"I love you."

"I love you, Mandy. More than you'll ever know."

They didn't say the words to each other often enough, but if he had to face whatever hostility was out there in Crumpton, she didn't want him leaving without knowing it from her. He reached down took her by her waist, touched his beautifully rounded pink lips to hers, and made her insides go all melty and cold at the same time.

Dear God, don't ask me to do without him. Please.

When he let her go, Amanda's skirts swung a bit like a bell. They had an audience of Isaac, who had a stormy look on his face, Lucy and Robert Lakey. Her handsome husband swung up on Isaac's gray dapple, and they rode off, nodding at the visiting white people as fast as the horses could carry them in the direction of Crumpton.

Stay strong.

They were his last words, almost, and she would hold onto them.

"Is March all right? We came to see about the dear child." Lucy stepped up onto her porch.

She hadn't invited her, but maybe she should have since they had been working together. "She's sleeping. I tried to fix her something to eat, but she just wanted to sleep."

"Bless her. I would have taken care of her while you were gone, if you had wanted me to."

Amanda shook her head at the implication that Isaac was somehow responsible for all of this. "She's fine. I appreciate the offer of help, but she's fine."

"So why are your husband and Isaac riding away as if the wind could carry them off? Did she get lost, or did someone take her?" Robert's face webbed in confusion.

Interesting. Now that Virgil was gone, she could see something of what her husband saw in her old school chum. Still, until they could find Tom Dailey's body for themselves, it was best to keep things quiet. For March's sake.

"She got lost in the woods. Dear thing, she was trying to come to find us. She wanted to go on a honeymoon too. Sounded like a sweet time. She likes candy, you know."

Robert laughed. "I know. Giving her candy is the quickest way to get her to do anything."

Amanda wasn't sure what that meant, but she folded her hands and smiled, satisfied she had told truth enough to suffice. For now.

Lucy spoke up. "I've been wanting to talk with you for a while now since the courthouse. I wonder if this is still a good time."

She wrinkled her brow at Lucy. What could she possibly mean? "Certainly. What may I help you with?"

"Well, Robert and I have been talking."

"Robert, is it?" Amanda's eyebrows raised up.

"Well, Mr. Lakey."

"Oh, there's no use trying to outsmart old Stew. She could see it right away that I took a liking to you, Lucy."

"And I you, Mr. Lakey."

"Yes. Virgil and I had suspected that love was in the air around here."

"Mrs. Milford and I are going to be married, Stew."

She nodded. "I'm glad to hear that Robert. Milford is a Christian community."

"We would like your husband to perform the ceremony."

Amanda quirked an eyebrow. A black man, marrying a white couple? Well, this was a new day indeed. Her voice carried calm in it. "I'm sure he would be honored."

"Wonderful. And Stew, Lucy and I have talked. About the school."

She took in a deep breath. So much of her dream had to be on the back burner. Family came first. If the events of the past few weeks taught her anything, it had certainly taught her that. "I know you've been letter writing to see about a church in Ohio that might help sponsor the school. Who knows when that's going to come through?"

"Don't get so discouraged, Stew. It's coming. People in Ohio know of you, and they'll be willing to help. You'll see."

"Thank you, Robert. But soon, I'm going to have to leave Milford with my family. I'll be moving Milford College to Atlanta."

Robert and Lucy looked at one another, and Lucy's blue eyes went wide with horror. "What about your efforts here?"

"I don't know. I won't be able to do both. I've come to see that now. I'll restart my efforts in Atlanta. There are people who need education there as well."

"But what about the Baxters? Don't they need education? You've worked awfully hard, Stew—to come so far."

"Well, it seems like the best solution. We don't have the big house anymore, and there isn't a new building. Virgil has a new opportunity. All signs seem to be pointing away from here."

"Just because you don't have the house anymore isn't a reason to give up." Lucy insisted.

Lucy's previously quiet and gentle demeanor seemed stirred up, and Mandy didn't know whether to laugh or frown at this new interference.

"We would need funds to build a new building and that will take time," she pointed out.

"Well, this sheds a new light on things, for sure." Lucy guided herself to one of the chairs on the porch and sat down, looking stunned. "I suppose the school is yours, but Robert thought…"

"What Lucy is trying to say, Stew, is that Lucy and I wanted to watch over the school for you while you were in Atlanta. There's no need to move it away from where it is doing good here. Atlanta is a large city, and I'm sure that there are opportunities for the people there for school. You might even start a branch there if you wanted to. But, don't take Milford College from Milford. It belongs here."

"You. And Lucy."

"Yes. We're quite resolved. You seemed to be, as well, we just never thought you would think of moving the school away . . ."

No, she never had either. Until she came to understand she had sacrificed a great deal for the school. Maybe too much. Now it was her turn to sacrifice for her family. Only, maybe God had provided a way . . .

Lucy fixed her eyes on her. "Please don't take the school. It's the first thing I've been able to do on my own that was meaningful."

"Would Robert mind if you taught after you married?"

Robert laughed and reached out to Lucy, and they clasped hands, standing next to one another. "Don't you remember how much we had talked up the Seneca Falls Convention of '48? Lucy and I will be together and will take care of things together. The stronger the school is, the better. And you'll be welcome back to see all of the proceedings whenever you want and to check on things anytime you want. We aren't kicking you out, you know."

"I appreciate that." She gave a wry smile. "And I never knew the school was meaningful for you as well."

"Clara thinks me foolish, but these days," Lucy drew close to Robert. "I care less for what Clara thinks. She's my sister, not my mother."

"Jack's going to help as long as his assignment will let him, as well. Old Milford College is in good hands, Stew."

"Well, I will have to pray about this, but . . . looking at the way that you are holding hands, I would say that the sooner that my husband returns and gets some rest, the sooner the marriage ceremony can be performed."

Lucy flashed her a beautiful smile. "I couldn't be happier. And please, don't worry about the things for the school. I've made it clear that if we need my portion of the house to have class until a building can be built, all the better."

"That does sound like an answer to prayer indeed." She stuck her hands in her pockets. There was no hugging them, so it was just best to thank them. "Thank you so very much. For everything."

Lucy stood closer to Robert. "I should be thanking you, Amanda. I lived in fear that I would be spending the rest of my days drifting, while being waited on hand and foot. It's so much better to have a vocation and a purpose in life. And there is so much work to be done here."

Robert picked up his future wife's hand. "Stew, the day you sent for me was one of the happiest days of my life. Some at Oberlin didn't like you because of your skin tone, but I'm so glad God blessed you with your dusky hue. I would have never known you and would not have had the opportunity to come to the barbaric south to meet the future Mrs. Robert Lakey."

"It's a blessing from God for me too, Robert, trust me. Thank you both. I'll let you know when Virgil returns and we can make arrangements."

"If March is up to it, I would like her to sing," Lucy peered over her shoulder trying to see if March was up.

"We can discuss that as well, when she awakes and is all better."

"We'll leave you to care for her. Thank you." Lucy was about to step away, but Amanda held up her hand.

She had to thank them in some way and she could only think of one way.

"I've been rather occupied over the past few weeks, but if you want to stay and share in some breakfast, I would be honored."

Robert and Lucy eyed one another. "Stew is just one of the best cooks ever," Robert said, "Kept me alive through college, I will say."

"Thank you, for your kind invitation."

For the first time, Lucy Milford stepped across the threshold of the Smithson home. She invited friends into her home, ones that would want to help her with her dream of Milford College. A warm glow suffused her at the sight of March sleeping, and the couple who moved quietly into the dining room of her home to share a meal with her. One more prayer remained.

Please God. Keep my husband safe in your care. Amen.

"If I ever hear any more talk about you going back to Africa, I'ma make it happen myself."

Virgil and Isaac had ridden much of the toll road in the early morning quiet for a very long time. Despite the dark events of the previous days, it was a beautiful morning, and Virgil wanted to rejoice in the splendor of it, but several things disturbed his soul in what his child had told them.

Isaac jerked himself up in the saddle. "March must have misunderstood. I never said that."

"I'm hoping so. You know she sees things kind of and she got a tender heart, so you might have said something that made her think that's what you wanted."

"That child is something. I said nothing."

The quiet rested between them again. "You would tell me if you was thinking 'long them lines though?"

"I'm about getting tired of you Smithson people. Isn't that what I said?"

"I need you here, Isaac. These times need you. The smithy, the town while we are gone, we need you."

"So you leaving?"

"Soon as I can get my family packed to go."

"Won't be any fun without you all around."

"Don't need fun. This here is a new day, require new responsibilities. Yours is the smithy and the town. Got it?"

"I got it. Don't worry."

"One of the friends of the young Baxter girls might get some ideas on you now about matching you up with a friend."

His friend jerked himself up even more. "Ain't looking for that."

"I just wanted to put that out there, so you remember Milford's a Christian community."

Isaac's dark brown features froze. He knew his friend's pain was real. "I may not preach, but I know that, Virgil."

"Many of these young friends of our nieces tried to throw themselves in my path, when Sally died and I had March by myself. Lot of them is related to one another, and there aren't many menfolk from outside the Baxter clan, so . . . that's why it be a shame for the school to go. Really, it's one chance for new blood to come to town."

"Where the school going?"

"With Mandy. To Atlanta."

"That's a shame. Pauline, I mean she would want me to continue my schooling."

"I would too, but it can't be helped, I suppose." He turned his horse sharply onto the faded trail that traced the edge of the inlet into the deeper woods. "Here's where we were this morning."

"Thick woods here."

"Yes. I don't know how she got herself back in here."

"You said Dailey brought her back in here."

He gripped the reins tighter into his fist. "That's what she say."

"When I get my hands on him . . ."

"Hey." Virgil pulled up and stopped, and Isaac stopped next to him. "He's mine. I'm the law around here, and like I told you before . . . I'ma take care of this."

"He mighta stole off your daughter, but he killed my wife." His friend's pained voice oozed through his own clenched teeth, not wanting to make noise. People lived this deep in the woods, and Virgil knew two Negroes on horseback this early in the morning didn't look like they were doing the right kind of fishing.

"I heard that. Pauline was a pillar of the community. But you got too much emotion tied up in this."

"And you don't?" Isaac gazed at Virgil's balled up fist. Virgil turned the horse away from his friend and continued down the path. He had a point. *God, please help me when the time comes. Help me to know what to do, what to say, and how to be. How to be like your son when he died for us on the cross making the greatest sacrifice of them all. For all of us. In your name. Amen.*

He should have prayed with Isaac. But he didn't. There was so much in his heart just now; he couldn't appear too open, even to his friend. Mandy had a point. There was sacrifice. Then just when it seemed too much to bear….

"I'm going to start looking in these boathouses. Watch out for anyone else and don't do nothing, less you hear shooting."

His friend shifted in his saddle, nodding.

Fortunately, the first couple of boathouses didn't have boats in them, so they were easy to inspect.

The fourth boathouse had a boat in it, so he had to get on board to see who was on the boat. Pistol prepared and held before him, he checked every compartment and crevice. Nothing.

There were only two more boathouses to inspect in this part of the shore, but his blood stirred up already. At his daughter this time. What did she mean by Dailey not moving? Was he dead? And if he were dead, then what did that mean for March staying in Milford? What was the law on child murderers in his town? He couldn't say. All he could say is he would leave and take his family as far away as he could. He would protect March and Mandy with all he had in him.

When he came out of that boathouse to get to the next one, he saw the disappointed look on Isaac's face. "Only two more left."

"I'm still waiting on you. Out here."

His friend's pain at not being allowed first crack at Dailey was obvious by the impatient way he kept moving in his saddle. Obvious enough that he didn't need to say anything.

Entering the next boathouse where a fine-fishing schooner was kept, he paused. He didn't recognize the schooner, but it was a beautiful boat. He boarded it and ducked into the bedroom of the boat. Nothing.

A click sounded in the still of the early morning and a fist of fear grabbed at his stomach.

"What you doing here? Thought you was off honeymooning with your smart pretty Yankee gal."

Virgil turned seeing Dailey pointed a gun at him. "Had to come back. I heard tell you stole my little girl off the highway."

"I didn't take no pickaninny off of the road. She come with me."

"You call her a liar?"

"I told her I would help her find you."

"What you coming back in this woods with her for then?"

"Well, I told her we could take a boat up to Atlanta."

"Ain't no boats going to Atlanta."

"Not my fault she don't know her geography."

Dailey's gun trained on him, but God help him; there was nothing in front of him but iron-red rage like his forge. He lunged on Tom Dailey like a mountain cat, and the gun clattered to the floor, going off into a doorframe of the boat.

Kneeling over his smelly, disgusting prey, he pushed his fist down into Dailey's face over and over again until he saw nothing but black and red all mixed together in the blood-saturated mess he made of Dailey's already ugly features.

CHAPTER TWENTY

"Get him, Virgil! Get him good!"

Isaac's enthusiastic cheering for his most unpreacher-like behavior called him to himself.

"Where're the horses? Thought I told you to watch them."

"Tied them up. And I did hear the gun go off?"

Dailey's gun. Virgil got up and pointed to the pistol, and Isaac took it up.

Dailey spat some teeth onto the ground through the hole that was his mouth once upon a time. "I didn't lay a finger on your child."

"That's for her to say. I beat you up for killing Pauline. If you laid a hand on my child, I would have shot you, so you could get to the gates of hell that much faster."

"Everything I done for you." Dailey spat. "Getting to be a fine politician."

His eyes gleamed. "You own a business. Everything I done was a fair exchange. You know you wouldn't be able to be elected anything."

"That's right. I put my money on a winning horse. But I can always stable you, boy, when I feel like it."

Virgil leaned down into Dailey's drunken, messed-up face. "I'm a man. And don't call my daughter a pickaninny either. I've held Isaac back from letting loose on you, and if you keep on being hateful, I might let him do what he wants."

Dailey's blue eyes fixed on Isaac, who stood just behind Virgil and said nothing.

Virgil and Isaac turned to get off the boat and got back on their horses.

"Guess he wasn't dead." Isaac's entire posture was downcast.

"No, Just terribly drunk." Part of what Virgil felt was a relief. Still, in his very drunken state, who knew what he did to March? *God, please let her be okay.*

He said nothing to Isaac, who had the care of March while he was away and blamed himself. It took a while for him to find his own head again after Sally had died, and he shouldn't have forced the care of a precocious little girl on him in the early stages of grief. Still, as they rode back to Milford on the backs of their fast-paced horses, he couldn't help but realize—it was time for them to leave and make a home elsewhere. Time to take March somewhere to be protected, as she deserved. How could he ever ask her the questions to find out what had happened on that boat with Tom Dailey? He had to be satisfied he had taken his revenge.

He only hoped Mandy would be able to understand why they had to leave Milford just now. She wouldn't like it, but he was her husband, and she had vowed to obey him in all things.

For the first time in a long time, he felt a little like laughing. Getting Mandy to obey? Mandy's strong Christian character meant she would remember her wedding vows and do as he required.

The reins felt smooth in his hand instead of wrinkled. What a blessing. He urged the horse on to go faster once they hit the toll road. He had to have Mandy in his arms again.

The wedding day of Lucy and Robert reminded Amanda of the June day two years before when she stood under the tree with Virgil and promised to take a strange man as her husband and his beautiful child as her own daughter. This June day, almost two years to the day, dawned just as hot and bright. *Maybe it's a good omen for them.*

She hoped so. It was a good omen for the school to celebrate another pairing, another couple uniting their lives in Christian love once more.

Lucy and Robert wanted to be married under the tree in the same way, but Virgil nixed that idea—without explaining why. Amanda readied the basket of food to take for the picnic reception, and she smiled to herself. How amazing it was the future Mr. and Mrs. Lakey had integrated themselves so completely into the community that they wanted to be married as the slaves were married. No, she agreed with her husband. Some customs were meant to be preserved as is. Milford Christian Church would do fine for them.

The reception picnic would be held in front of the Milford house, since absolutely no one felt like frolicking in the town square, even though, due to Amanda and

March's love and care, the flowers had started to bloom again. The only factor missing would be Clara Milford. She had become incredibly jealous of her sister-in-law and had done everything to discourage her from marrying Robert Lakey. When she saw the way the winds were blowing, Clara declared Lucy as the caretaker of her part of the house and went back to Tennessee on the train three days before. Jack Kirchner seemed disappointed, but Clara's abrupt departure a few weeks ago soothed Amanda's prayerful heart.

No one had stepped forward to own the burning of the town square, but ever since she had brought it back to life, nursing the blooms on her hands and knees with March beside her, she had her suspicions about who had done the evil deed. Clara had to go. There was so much love in Milford, and Lucy had found her own strength and voice, that someone like Clara felt uncomfortable in staying.

Jack Kirchner stayed on, willing to help do the work of the Freedman's Bureau he was appointed to do, but Amanda had the feeling if Clara had stayed, there might have been some suspiciously less than Christian behavior sparked between them. That wouldn't do. So Clara had to go on back home to her Tennessee family and be satisfied with her funds sent to her regularly from her sister-in-law.

"All set?"

She looked up to witness the sight of her husband, dressed in his best black broadcloth suit, so handsome, ready to perform the marriage ceremony. "I am. And may I say you look wonderful."

Virgil rarely smiled, but Amanda knew he was on the edge of doing it. "You're the one who is beautiful, my lovely wife."

"I do my best to look good next to you."

"You'll outshine them all in Atlanta."

When he said that this time, her heart didn't sink as it had before. She had made her peace with it. She just handed him a basket. "Put this in the back of the wagon. March will watch over everything."

"She upstairs?"

"Yes." She gathered up the pink sprigged material in her hand to go retrieve March from her room where she had been dressing. They were less inclined to let her go off into the woods, and it was a good thing, because now, March was less inclined to go, making for a new change in the behavior of the little girl.

"Ready, March?"

March turned, dressed in a new white dress Amanda had made for the special occasion. It fit her perfectly, which meant that March's legs looked less spindly and her arms less gawky. "I am. Thank you."

"Let's go then, child."

When she came to Amanda, she gave her daughter a squeeze and guided her to the door. They gathered up the last of the items and loading up, the Smithsons made their way to the Milford's front yard for the wedding and on to the church in the town square. Every soul in the hamlet was turned out for the wedding day in the church, and the church was just as packed as it was for Pauline's funeral.

It wasn't every day that Milford's current white denizens got married. Including Franklin Jr., of course. He and March were the wedding party, and everyone oohed and ahhed as she helped to walk him down the aisle of the church. Amanda gladly took little Franklin on her lap to watch over him while his mother became Mrs. Robert Lakey.

There had been a lot of discussion as to who would guide Lucy down the aisle. She decided, as was her right as a married lady, to walk down by herself to her new husband. "I'm not a maiden virgin," she explained and it all made wonderful sense.

A feeling of peace and love came over her as she watched her old college chum be married. Lucy's pale features were illuminated by the oyster gray dress that she wore, and her face framed by a new soft gray bonnet, a perfect wedding outfit for a war widow.

Franklin squirmed a bit in Amanda's arms, but when March stepped forward to sing, by herself, the baby quieted. March sang *The Lord's Prayer*, set to a tune she created. There wasn't a dry eye in the house. Where had these talents come from? Where had she learned to do that?

When she finished, she sat down next to her mother, and Amanda dropped a kiss on March's forehead, pulling her into her embrace.

The loud raucous party in front of the Milford farmhouse made for a wonderful celebration. It was a celebration that they were all there, all alive, all on the verge of change. Her midsection ached in pain at thinking about Pauline again. Seeing Virgil talking to some constituents, and March playing a quiet game with some girls, she slipped away to the slave cemetery on the far side of the house.

Pauline's grave, marked with the beautiful iron rose bouquet Isaac made for her, shone bright and new where the red dirt was beginning to grow over with grass and flatten again. Then, out of the corner of her eye, something in the cemetery sparkled.

It was an engraving of a baby cradle forged in polished iron, and she read a name engraved in the circlet placed in the ground. "Lawrence Virgil Smithson. A light too soon dimmed."

When had this gotten here? Had Virgil put it here? Tears blurred her vision and made the circlet dance in front of her eyes. Her vision clouded so she didn't see her husband standing at the edge of the gate that marked off the graves, black apart from white.

"Did you put this here?" Amanda whipped a hanky out from her pocket and wiped the freshet of tears away.

"Mandy. You know I'm not the best artist in the world with that iron. I'm just good at making horseshoes."

She sat back from him and made a face, and he grabbed her encircling her in his hold. She leaned back in it, feeling comforted, as she always did, by his close embrace. "Okay. Did you have Isaac make it?"

"That's the question. I did."

"Thank you."

"You're welcome."

"It comforts me knowing there's something here, as if we haven't left him behind."

"We going to be back, Mandy. Milford's our home. Ain't no one keeping us from our home."

"I appreciate that clarity, husband. I really do."

"I'm glad you have less worry about the school now, and when we come on back, it's going to be bigger and better."

"And Virgil. Please, I want to say thank you to you for taking this service on."

"No thanking needed."

"I think it is. It's a lot of sacrifice and I'm proud of you for doing it for our people."

"Well when you put it that way . . ."

She laughed and he squeezed her. They stood there, looking at the small place where their son laid to rest. Turning about in his secure hold, she touched her lips to his and he kissed her, making her lips melt against his, warm and willing. He couldn't pull on her braids, as she might like, since they were up in her chignon, but his touch made her tingle just the same. Besides, he could do it later on when they were alone. "I love you, Mrs. Smithson."

"And I you, husband. Always. Help me from here."

He offered her the crook of his arm out to her and she put her hand there, relishing in the steel-strong security of his arm.

This is what mattered. This is what counted. The creation of a family that would be her strength. God saw to that. It was his blessing to her.

Virgil turned to her. "When we didn't know where March was, that was just about the worst. To have someone we loved so much, be in danger or fear, it was too much. I have to pray to God, but sometimes, my faith is weak in bringing another child into this world and going through that some more. But if it's what you want, wife—I'll be there for you."

She warmed, feeling as if she swallowed the sun. “Let’s talk about it further. After the wedding party is over. When we say a temporary goodbye to the bed you carved that’s in our bedroom.”

“I don’t know how I’m going to make it happen, but that bed is coming to Atlanta with us. I’m not sleeping on some strange boarding house bed.”

She squeezed his arm. “I’m so glad to hear you say that, husband. Very glad indeed.”

The sun in her heart told her God had already blessed her. Many times over. Even though these were hard times, He would bless her many times more. With Virgil and March by her side, she would have strength, love, and patience enough to discover those blessings, one day at a time.

AUTHOR'S NOTE

I hope that you enjoyed *The Mayor's Mission*! If you enjoyed the continuing love story of Virgil and Amanda, please return to your place of purchase on-line and leave a review. I love to hear from you!

The complicated politics of the Reconstruction Era varied wildly between the former Confederate states. Georgia was one of the states where some progressive things happened but some other advances were taken away. What happened when those opportunities were taken away is the concern of the next story in "The Founder's Trilogy" of the "Home to Milford College" series—*The Representative's Revolt.*

Take a moment to visit me at my blog where I will continue to discuss my writing and research twice a month at http://piperhuguley.com. There you can find posts about some of the real people who appear in the stories, like Henry McNeal Turner and Tunis Campbell, and you may sign up for my mailing list to be kept informed of my releases.

In the meantime, if you are curious, here are some of the resources that I used to research *The Mayor's Mission:*

Angell, Stephen. *Bishop Henry McNeal Turner and African-American Religion in the South*

Drago, Edmund. *Politicians and Reconstruction: A Splendid Failure*

DuBois, W.E.B. *Black Reconstruction in America 1860-1880*

Duncan, Russell. *Freedom's Shore: Tunis G. Campbell and the Georgia Freedmen*

Edgerton, Douglas. *The Wars of Reconstruction: A Brief Violent History of America's Most Progressive Era*

Foner, Eric. *Reconstruction*

Thompson, C. Mildred. *Reconstruction in Georgia.*

Coming Spring 2015
The Representative's Revolt

If they can't get the newly elected representatives out by legal means, then they'll kill them, one by one....
Virgil Smithson is at the top of the list.

Atlanta, Georgia, 1871
Someone has tried to assassinate Virgil Smithson. The Georgia State Legislature is not a safe place—if it ever was. To protect her growing family, Amanda wants to go home to Milford. Virgil is willing to serve out his term and return to life as a blacksmith, but first he has to know...who is trying to have him killed?

Meanwhile, Amanda works to resolve Milford College's everlasting financial woes by starting a fund raising campaign to finish the school building. Her efforts require her absence from home and the many pressures influence the marriage of the Milford College founders.

Then, a missive arrives from Ohio and Amanda receives an offer she feels she cannot refuse.

When all they want is what they had in the first place, a quiet life in Milford, Virgil and Amanda must strengthen their faith to negotiate these difficult days of the Reconstruction Era.

Someone is trying to put an end to the dream of Milford College and Virgil Smithson's life. In this, the finale of the "Founder's Trilogy" the Representative and his wife have to find a way to figure it all out...before it's too late.

CHAPTER TWENTY-TWO

Piper Huguley is the author of the "Home to Milford College" series. The series traces the love stories at a small "Teachers and Preachers" college in Georgia over time, beginning with the love story of the founders. Book one in the series, *The Preacher's Promise*, was a semi-finalist in Harlequin's So You Think You Can Write contest, and a quarter-finalist in the 2014 Amazon Breakthrough Novel Award contest. The next entry, which continues Virgil and Amanda's love story, *The Representative's Revolt*, will be published in Spring 2015.

Huguley is also the author of "Migrations of the Heart," a five-book series of inspirational historical romances set in the early 20th century featuring African American characters. Book one in the series, *A Virtuous Ruby,* will be published by Samhain Publishers in July 2015.

Piper Huguley blogs about the history behind her novels

at http://piperhuguley.com. She lives in Atlanta, Georgia with her husband and son.

Books by Piper Huguley
The Lawyer's Luck
The love story of Amanda Smithson's parents
Available in print and on Kindle, Nook, Kobo and iTunes.

The Preacher's Promise
Where it all started for Virgil and Amanda Smithson
Available in print and on Kindle.